More Fool Me

C.L. Jennison

To all the women who have shocking stories to tell about despicable men

Deception comes in many forms.
It's even more destructive when delivered by a familiar hand.
— Descent into Deceit

Establishing Intimacy

It was the murky, early days of online dating, when people were still suspicious of the 'desperate' few who met that way, intensifying the need for secrecy. It was difficult for her to remember not having instantaneous access to everything, but nobody did back then and sending and receiving emails was a novelty rather than a chore or an intrusion.

They had exchanged hundreds of them, then instant messages, then texts, before she finally agreed to meet him face to face, in a remote pub car park, without telling anyone else, against all the warnings about where was safe for young women to meet strangers. But he wasn't a stranger by then. The intimacy had been established and embedded through affectionate terms of endearments and she wasn't afraid in the slightest. Quite the opposite, in fact.

He was tall, dark, handsome and well built – skinny men didn't do it for her at all – and wore designer labels, a black leather jacket and a black cap to their arranged rendezvous. A wolf in wolf's clothing.

'Hello, m'lady,' he said, grinning, using the title he had created for her, verbally branding her as his straight away.

He was sexy as hell, and she knew immediately she was hopelessly infatuated.

Their first date didn't end. Those first few hours merged seamlessly into several nights and days in a row. It happened as naturally as a developing photograph, their relationship gaining clarity with each passing moment until they were frozen in time, perfect for ever. Or so she thought.

She couldn't have been more wrong.

A few years later she finally fled from danger, from him, yet she was still trapped within the fragile yet impenetrable shell of the person she had become. That he had made her. He had poisoned her life more effectively than arsenic.

— *Descent into Deceit*

Chapter One

January 2017

As I type *The End*, emotion bubbles up within me and tears well in my eyes. I stare at my decrepit laptop screen in a shocked trance, at the final page of my completed manuscript. I'm "pleased as punch" as my grandpa used to say before his demons consumed him, yet I feel strangely spent and sombre at the same time. It's the classic book hangover, I tell myself, the inevitable bereft feeling when you return to reality after being immersed in a compelling story. Except this time the feeling is intensified as the supposed fictional characters have lived my truth, and the storyline was my real life. I've been reliving it all again these past few months; a masochistic yet cathartic project.

'Shall I tell the writing group my good news?' I ask Hardy, who is curled up on the floor by my chair as usual. He jerks his head up and cocks it to one side, which I take as a yes. Opening a new email and adding five addresses, I type one word in the subject line – *DONE!!!* – followed by one silly sentence:

```
Local author receives awards galore for
debut novel...
```

I smile, press send and sit back. I've achieved my New Year's resolution just three weeks into January, after promising myself months ago that 2017 would be the year I finally purged my painful past and put pen to paper, or fingertips to laptop keys. Now it's official.

Stretching like a cat, arms out in front of me, fingers intertwined backwards, I try to enjoy the dizzy, freeing feeling of finally finishing my manuscript for a few moments, before unclasping my fingers and sitting up again, loosening my neck and arching my back. As I do a sharp pain takes my breath away, and I press my palm to my ribcage tenderly. I screw my eyes shut and breathe slowly and deeply for a few moments, as I always do when this happens. It's never healed properly.

Gingerly, I stand and shuffle the short distance from my rickety desk to my galley kitchen to retrieve the treats I bought specially to mark the occasion, returning minutes later to notifications of three new emails. Sylvie, Joy and Kenny have already replied to my announcement. I sit down again to read them, and I'm overjoyed at their kind words; is this what it feels like to have a group of friends?

```
Sylvie:  Best  feeling  in  the  world!
Incredible  achievement.  Can't  wait  to
hear  all  about  it  on  Wednesday  —  it
might  even  spark  some  motivation  in
me! Xx


Joy:  Congrats,  darling!  Still  battling
with  all  three  of  mine,  as  you  well
know! X


Kenny: Well done, Paige. Knew you would
get there in the end. See you Wednesday.
```

As I smile at my screen, Hardy nuzzles my hand, wanting to be fussed over. I stroke his soft black and white fur, feeling a sudden burst of pride, and gratitude, for the life I now lead – dog-mum, business owner and now author, too! In my euphoria, I fleetingly consider messaging Julia, like I used to, but quickly think better of it. The past is best left in the past; it's time to try to concentrate on the future, if I can. If I can stay strong enough.

I fire off three quick thank you messages and return to the short but friendly email enquiry I received earlier today from an author named Aydan Keyes, who'd got my contact details from an acquaintance of an acquaintance, so he explained. I've practically committed the message to memory, but I read through it yet again, as well as my sent reply suggesting a meeting next week, obsessively checking I sound as professional, knowledgeable and cordial as possible. It's a big deal; he could potentially be my first proper proofreading client, not counting the mates' rates work I currently do for Joy (the rate being free as she hasn't actually paid me a penny yet!).

According to my frequently updated finance spreadsheet, I should have enough money left from my inheritance, after selling Grandpa's bungalow in Grimsby and buying this modest two-bed terrace near Hull's city centre, to last maybe another year, if I continue to be as careful as I have been. But I really need, and want, the business to take off so that my savings don't dwindle away to nothing. Now that I've moved on geographically, I need to finally move on mentally, too.

Finally closing my laptop, I gather my rare celebration collection from my desk – raspberry gin and elderflower tonic to drink and Ben and Jerry's cookie dough ice cream to eat – and retire to my second-hand yet comfortable sofa for an evening of pure escapism watching *The Shining*. From now on this will always be my end of manuscript ritual, I decide.

Settling down with Hardy at my side and the Overlook

Hotel looming ominously on the screen, I am once again absorbed by Jack Torrance's descent into madness, and now feel wryly empathetic given my own intense novel-writing experience. I finally toast myself and my achievement. Sylvie was right: it is indeed the best feeling in the world.

Suddenly, a car horn blasts outside and Hardy jolts up, almost knocking the ice cream tub out of my hand. He leaps off the sofa and scampers out of the room to the small hallway, tail up and ears back, his rumbling growl becoming a frenzied bark, his claws tap-tap-tapping on the badly fitted laminate flooring as he spins in agitated circles, ready to confront the perceived threat. My constant protector.

I open the half glass lounge door wider and enter the hallway too. As I approach the front door, I vocalise my reassurances, as much for myself as for Hardy. Without turning the light on, I take a shaky breath and force myself to peel back the curtain and peek out through the left-hand narrow window panel. My nose is barely an inch from the glass as I scope out the street, but all I can see is my usual view: the opposite row of terraced houses stretching left and right, behind the permanent rows of cars parked bumper to bumper on both sides of the road. Between them, a Ford Fiesta XR2 idles with its stereo now blaring – the cause of all the noise.

Satisfied that there's nothing untoward to be concerned about, I automatically double-check the door is locked, even though I know for sure it already is. Just as I'm about to tug the curtain closed, I hear an even louder squall of music as the XR2's passenger opens the door and emerges, slamming the door behind them and squeezing through two parked cars to get to the pavement. It looks like a man. Reaching the house opposite mine, he leans against its low wall, crosses his legs at the ankles, and lights up a cigarette. Positioned in the shadows just beyond the street lamp's glow, his exhaled smoke dances up towards the light and I squint, unable to see much more than his outline. Even though I know he can't see me, I'm aware I'm trembling while a still-grumbling Hardy sniffs around the letter box at the bottom of our door.

A few moments later the man flicks his cigarette onto the ground and pulls something from his pocket. As he moves towards the light, I see that he's holding a cap and as he pulls it on and sets off purposely down the street, the street lamp illuminating his black leather jacket, the memory blindsides me like a mugger at midnight.

Just like that, I'm catapulted back there, to the past. The logical part of my brain takes a back seat and I let go of the door curtain as though it's scalded me, scrambling backwards towards the stairs. I sit on the second scuffed step, my socked feet on the battered laminate, and curl in on myself as Hardy fusses round me, trying to offer supportive licks and wet nose nudges. My ribcage throbs in protest, and I feel like screaming. Instead, I whisper three things, the repeated mantra I've been telling myself for just over three years, every time something like this happens:

'It's not him. He doesn't know where I live. He's still locked up.'

Chapter Two

Wednesdays always roll around so quickly, probably because I look forward to them so much. I'm even more excited today as I know I'm going to be made a fuss of at the writing group meeting due to finally finishing my manuscript last week. Although I don't normally favour being the centre of attention, I can't help but be childishly gleeful about it. My writing friends are the only ones who really understand the sense of pride I'm currently feeling. It's been so long since I had anything to feel proud of myself for, it's practically intoxicating.

We began hosting the writing groups at each other's houses on a rota basis after our original venue – an independent coffee shop in the city's popular Newland Avenue – closed its doors a few weeks ago. I'm relieved; although the coffee shop was small, it was still a public place, so my anxiety is greatly minimised by our new arrangement.

I'm also relishing the opportunity to get out of my own head for a couple of hours. My masochistic brain has been replaying distressing scenes from the past since mine and Hardy's fright on Friday night, sending me into something of an emotional slump despite my well-worn coping mechanisms. It's probably an inevitable consequence of finishing the book, I grimly admit. After all, I've effectively lived through the horror twice now so it's no wonder I'm jumpier than usual.

Just before 10am, I pull up outside Sylvie's grand house in Hessle at the same time as Renee. She waits for me on the tree-lined pavement at the end of Sylvie's long private driveway, looking decidedly irked. After greeting each other we fall in step as we walk across the white gravel towards the front door.

'Everything okay?' I ask.

'Nothing an empty nest won't solve.' She tuts and shakes her head, her shoulder-length frizzy hair acting as an external indication of her inner exasperation. 'Honestly, I know some parents dread their children leaving home, but I can't wait. I feel like I'm an unpaid – and overworked – receptionist, cleaner and psychologist all rolled into one. Geoff and Alexander had yet another blazing row this morning, so I know Geoff's sick and tired of it all too. At this rate, Alexander's going to be knocking on forty by the time he finally sets up home elsewhere with whatever woman will put up with him!'

I grimace and make sympathetic noises, as much as I can as someone without any children, let alone a problematic grown-up son overstaying his welcome. However, as the youngest member of the writing group, hearing about family issues and troublesome offspring is not as commonplace as I expected. When I first joined the group last August, I worried that a few of the other members might start to see me as a surrogate daughter or niece with there being at least twenty years' difference between us. However, those are definitely not roles I wish to play – being a granddaughter was tough enough. Thankfully, everyone keeps themselves to themselves for the most part, which suits me perfectly. There's only Renee and Joy

I've bonded with beyond writing-related talk – on their side mostly, not mine.

Renee glances at me slyly as we reach Sylvie's arched outer door. 'How are things going with you anyway, Paige? Any interesting romantic prospects on the horizon?' she asks with what I infer as an underlying glimmer of hope that I could be the one to solve her Alexander problem, even though she certainly hasn't sold him as an appealing prospect.

I laugh at the barely disguised implication behind her question. 'No romantic prospects whatsoever. I am extremely happily single, thank you very much,' I report firmly. I don't share that the thought of trusting another man again still seems virtually impossible.

She smiles sheepishly in response as I press the doorbell. As the chimes sound, Renee touches my arm to get my attention again. 'Oh, by the way, well done on finally finishing your manuscript, you clever thing you.'

Before I get the chance to thank her, the door is flung open by our hostess and we fix the smiles to our faces. To me, Sylvie is even more gorgeous and glamorous than Helen Mirren, yet I don't believe she comes close to the Hollywood actress in the charisma stakes. Flustered yet haughty seems to be her default setting, which she demonstrates effectively as she ushers us through the porch and into the spacious hallway whilst simultaneously smoothing her sophisticated silver bob and apologising profusely for the 'mess'. Sylvie's double-fronted Georgian house is picture-perfect inside and out, yet to her critical eye there is always something to be fixed or changed or redecorated. I understood quickly after meeting her that Sylvie, the founder of our writing group, is an extremely lonely woman and consequently, the other members make indulgent allowances for her. I do now too.

'What mess?' asks Renee as Sylvie closes the inner door

behind us. 'Don't be silly, Sylvie, this beats my overcrowded living quarters any day!'

Sylvie smiles tightly to accept the compliment but doesn't dispute the statement, and Renee instantly looks a bit forlorn. Although, having been there, describing Renee's house as overcrowded is putting it mildly – it's cluttered and cramped and claustrophobic, and having known Renee for a few months now, I doubt that would change when – or if – Alexander does move out. Still, Sylvie could have responded more politely. Like I said: allowances.

Kenny and Lloyd are already seated around the table in Sylvie's large kitchen diner with Belinda Penfold, a rare special guest. They're all sipping coffee, clearly freshly poured from the giant cafetière sitting between them.

'Here she is – our author extraordinaire!' announces Lloyd as I walk in, and he stands up to clap. Everyone joins in, giving me a gentle round of applause, except Sylvie who is busying herself fussing over something on the kitchen island. I surprise myself by curtseying in response and blush, secretly thrilled at the recognition.

Sylvie bustles over and starts handing out printed agendas to us all. 'Yes, well done, Paige, as I said in my email on Friday. Now the hard work really starts with the dreaded revision process; everyone knows first drafts need serious triaging. But enough of that for the moment, we've got quite a packed meeting today!' Agendas distributed, she sits in her usual spot at the head of the table, her response quite at odds with her congratulatory email last week. I don't take offence; this is standard Sylvie.

'First things first, Joy can't make it today due to a prior family commitment, so I'll be sure to email her the minutes afterwards. Now, although our special guest Belinda isn't a writer, she's here to tell us all about a very special writing event!' Sylvie announces grandly and pauses for the obligatory curious sounds and expressions, which we all provide as though trained animals responding to our mistress's commands. 'You all know Belinda, don't you?' she hurriedly questions, looking around nervously in case she has to stop full flow excitement mode and back-pedal. She is visibly relieved when everyone nods, forgetting that we all met event planner Belinda at a small local poetry reading she organised a few weeks ago. Scatty Sylvie, I think, unkindly.

'Right, good, well then, I'll hand over to Belinda so she can explain more.'

Belinda smiles, adjusts her purple cat-eye glasses and glances down at her notebook, which is as pristine and sophisticated as she is – a leather Papier number. Never mind pets looking like their owners, I think notebooks perfectly reflect people's personalities. I look around the table to justify this philosophy and I'm pleased to see I'm right – our writer notebooks are well worn and dog-eared, full of ideas, scribbles and half-stories. No laptops or other technology here.

Renee's has a shabby cream cloth cover and sprayed gold edges, stuffed with extra bits of torn paper and held together with an elastic band, Lloyd's is a monogrammed moleskin journal, slight scuff marks around its soft corners, Kenny has a no-nonsense lined A4 writing pad, its bright orange 99p sticker starting to peel on the cover, and Sylvie has a fancy Filofax, creased after years of use but still enviable if you're a stationery obsessive like me.

I have a white hardback notebook covered in black polka dots – the first page showcases my neatest handwriting, but the following pages are covered in scruffy notes and crossings out and random sticky notes, the aim for perfectionism forgotten during the creative process. It's apt; 'it doesn't have to be perfect to be finished' was my mantra whilst writing my book.

I tune back into Belinda who is explaining the "very special writing event".

'...option to run a workshop at this year's book fair at the Guildhall as part of Hull's City of Culture programme of events, either one full day or separate morning and afternoon sessions of different groups, whichever you prefer.'

'What do we think?' asks Sylvie. 'When is it again?' she directs at Belinda before anyone has had a chance to answer.

'On Saturday the twelfth of March – just over six weeks from now.'

We all look at each other. Both Kenny and Renee take a sip of coffee and Belinda taps her expensive Parker pen against her page impatiently. Although I'm new to Hull, there's a real buzz about it being awarded City of Culture for 2017 and our little group being offered the opportunity to run a writing workshop is both an exciting and nerve-racking prospect. Although I'm not a published author yet, the idea does appeal greatly, even though I would personally prefer to stay hidden behind the scenes.

As always, one of us tests the water with a response to gauge Sylvie's reaction.

'I know I'm supposedly the traditional author,' Lloyd says, miming air quotes around the word 'traditional' as he is the only member so far to be published via a publishing house rather than being self-published, 'but that was years ago and I haven't written anything of note since, so I doubt I'd have any useful wisdom worth imparting right now.'

We all immediately jump to Lloyd's defence, although his negativity is all too familiar. He's been in the doldrums ever since the disappointingly mediocre sales of his second historical non-fiction book a couple of years ago following the success of his first. This led to his agent effectively dropping him, leaving him incredibly disillusioned with writing and publishing in general.

'Anyone else up for it?' asks Sylvie, interrupting our platitudes, obviously keen to return to the topic at hand, as per her printed agenda. 'It's a super publicity exercise for the group itself and may even prompt a few book sales for *all* of the published authors among us,' she states, looking pointedly at Lloyd and reminding everyone that her self-published book deserves as much recognition as his. Rightly so.

I clear my throat and Sylvie swings her gaze towards me. 'I'd like to be involved,' I venture timidly, quickly calculating the risk versus the reward in terms of potential knock-on paid proofreading work. I would be a fool not to offer despite my social anxiety. 'I know I'm not a published author in any capacity yet, but my professional proofreading training complements my personal writing experience and I'd be willing to have a go at helping put together a writing workshop.' I don't offer to deliver it though. The thought of addressing even a small group of strangers induces the familiar flutter of panic.

'You could use the same content for the morning and afternoon sessions if you wanted to split it for different cohorts,' says Belinda, thinking efficiently.

'Exactly!' booms Sylvie, clapping her hands together. 'We need to show we know our stuff and grow the group. Start small but who knows where it could lead?'

I smile and nod, amused at Sylvie's enthusiasm, and wonder how long it'll be before this "workshop malarkey" is riddled with "problems". Past experience has already taught me that the group trying anything new doesn't always live up to Sylvie's lofty expectations, and we soon return to the safety of our usual Wednesday morning meetings with no more said about it.

'Well, Paige, if you're offering to assemble the bones of the workshop, that's fine by me. Of course, I'm happy to play teacher on the day providing you send me everything to review beforehand,' states Sylvie, delegating all responsibility so expertly I barely register it.

'I'll help man the group's book stall, and I bet Joy will want to be involved with that too. She is the most prolific of all of us with three novels under her belt already,' says Renee.

'Three manuscripts,' distinguishes Sylvie spitefully. 'They're not published yet!'

Chapter Three

It's Thursday and my jean-clad knee jiggles with nerves as I wait in Starbucks along Clough Road for Aydan Keyes, my potential new proofreading client. Not being familiar with his choice of meeting place, and it being a bit further afield than I usually like to venture, I've arrived extra early. I collect my cappuccino – daubed *Page* rather than *Paige* – and take a prime viewing seat next to the rain-spattered façade of windows facing the busy road so I can try and spot him approaching.

However, due to not having any social media accounts, I haven't done what people usually do and searched for him online, so I don't know what he looks like. The blank spaces in place of any knowledge about him, other than he's written a book, are gaping holes for me to plummet through, if I let myself. I try to think calming, practical thoughts: this is a business meeting, he needs my help, and I need to build a reputation. Plus, there aren't many people here in this relatively out-of-the-way Starbucks, which helps to settle my social anxiety further. Be positive, Paige! I tell myself. This could be the start of an enjoyable and rewarding collaboration.

The ping of a notification disturbs my train of thought, and I take a quick sip of my drink before I open it. I'm already irrationally apprehensive in case it's Aydan emailing to cancel, meaning a wasted trip out of the safety of the house, leaving Hardy alone, and the loss of potential work. Peeking at my screen, I see it's not from Aydan, it's from Sylvie, and the dramatic, capitalised title *URGENT ACTION REQUIRED* is no doubt completely unwarranted. I open the email.

```
Following   yesterday's   meeting,   please
send  writing  workshop  ideas  for  review
ASAP.  As  discussed  yesterday,  as  the
founder  of  the  writing  group  and  a
published  author,  I  will  be  delivering
it.  It  is  my  neck  on  the  line  with
Belinda  and  I  can  advise  workshop
attendees  on  the  writing  and  publishing
process  from  start  to  finish  whereas
some  of  the  other  members  cannot.
However,  I  will  require  your  constant
support  on  the  day  please,  Paige.  Xx
```

I frown at both the demand and the implication behind her comments. Sylvie really is so superior at times. Yes, she is a published author, but by her own admission she is wallowing in obscurity following paltry book sales – a lot fewer than she expected. She and Lloyd actually have a lot in common in terms of languishing in the writing wilderness.

I throw my phone back in my bag in annoyance, irked at being distracted by a trivial email before my important meeting, and annoyed at myself for getting my hopes up about the writing workshop being a confidence-building experience in the first place. I really should have seen this coming. I know more than anyone that people can be wildly unpredictable. This is actually a timely reminder that I should be on my guard more; distasteful things can happen when you least expect them to.

As I often do, I think back to when I first joined the writing group last August, and the hopes I held in relation to it. For the previous seven months, since moving to Hull, I had kept myself securely squirrelled away, only popping out for essentials and to walk Hardy, trying to find a way to process my past and take charge of my life again following Grandpa's death. Caring for him for just over three years meant existing in a bubble, which I had welcomed at the time after having to leave Leeds so abruptly.

Becoming a freelance proofreader last year seemed a logical progression after working at *The Yorkshire Gazette* when I had lived in Leeds and it had two major draws: I didn't have to explain my career gap to anyone, and I could work from my new home – from the haven I created for myself. But I knew I needed a low-key network too, so when I saw a poster advertising the writing group in the library, I decided to stretch my comfort zone and join. As well as meeting authors that could become new proofreading clients or pass on my details to other authors they knew, I wanted some encouragement and accountability for my own novel-writing endeavour. So far, it's been just what I needed, Sylvie's maddening quirks aside.

A tall and lean but slightly buff bearded hipster type walks through the door of the coffee shop, and I know immediately that he's Aydan. He looks as nervous as I think I do. He glances around and we make eye contact, as though recognising each other. He points at me and mouths my name and I nod, too excessively. As he reaches me, I jump up like a Jack-in-the-box, accepting his quick formal handshake.

I momentarily regret my supposed professional yet informal choice of black jeans and a three-quarter sleeve plain white shirt, which I haven't worn since my *Gazette* days. I feel plain and dowdy in comparison to Aydan's casual, yet dapper, attire of ripped blue jeans and a blue T-shirt blanketed by a crew-neck cream jumper, sleeves pushed up to reveal tattooed forearms and braceleted wrists. He has a green canvas satchel slung over his shoulder but he's not wearing a coat despite the cold January weather. He smells and looks so clean and fresh and groomed he could be about to audition for a washing powder 'after' advert.

Based on our brief email exchanges, he's much more self-assured than I thought he would be and not what I expected at all – much younger for a start. He checks I'm okay for a drink then orders his at the counter while I try and compose myself.

A few minutes later, once he is settled in his seat, he slides his laptop out of his bag and sets it on the table between us. He scrolls through the first few chapters of his book – a non-fiction guide to property development – and then clicks open his accompanying chapter outline spreadsheet, with everything labelled and colour coded. I try not to show it but I am barely able to contain my glee at the opportunity to work with someone so clearly on my geeky wavelength. I acknowledge that appearances can sometimes be deceptive, in a good way.

The barista shouts his name and once he's back from collecting his cup of coffee, he frowns at his laptop then sighs in frustration.

'This book has driven me mad,' he confesses, running fingers decorated with silver rings through his trendy mullet. Practically hypnotised, I watch as it falls back exactly into place. 'I know what I want to say but getting the words down has been so hard and I'm not even writing a story, it's just a business strategy book. I don't know how proper writers do it.'

'If you're writing a book, you are a proper writer!' I say encouragingly. 'I'm a member of a writing group and we all know how hard it is no matter whether you're writing fiction or non-fiction. I've actually just finished writing my first novel,' I add, shyly, surprised at myself. It's been a long time since I shared personal details so readily with anyone, let alone a potential client.

'Really?' asks Aydan, his expression conveying both awe and admiration. 'What's it about?'

I hesitate, instantly unsure whether I'm ready to discuss the actual details of my book with a complete stranger. I've barely revealed any details to my writing group these past few months, despite their persistent curiosity. Yet Aydan's looking at me with such genuine interest that I find it difficult to resist not telling him about it and, if we're going to have a productive working relationship, I realise I probably need to open up a bit.

'It's a psychological thriller,' I finally reveal. I look down and tuck my hair behind my ear. 'It began as a mystery but morphed into something a bit darker and grittier.'

'So, you're like Agatha Christie with a twist?' he replies, becoming more animated. I look up at him again and his smile is lopsided and cute. 'I love those stories! A group of suspects, red herrings, seemingly impossible murders – they're great. I mostly listen to the audiobooks rather than read the physical books though, especially as I'm usually working on some building site or other. The stories keep me company while I break or fix things.'

I laugh at the image of a gorgeous hipster guy like Aydan listening to murder mystery audiobooks through his headphones, except he's quietly stirring his coffee, his lips pressed together.

'Oh. I'm sorry,' I say immediately, aware of his annoyance. 'I wasn't laughing at you, I think any form of reading is brilliant, you're just not exactly what I imagine when I think about Agatha Christie's ideal audience.' I'm aware I'm babbling, digging myself a deeper pit of shame and regret. Why do I always say the wrong thing? I'm so out of practice talking to anyone on a professional level.

'No, I'm sorry,' he replies, sitting back and softening his expression. 'You didn't do anything wrong, I'm just a bit sensitive about my dyslexia, hence the audiobooks. It means I can still access stories but on my limited terms.'

My skin prickles with embarrassment at my insulting inappropriateness, as well as with sympathy for his evident vulnerability.

'To be honest, I don't know how I've got this far through life – the illiterate property developer. Hey, that should be my book's title!' He half smiles, half grimaces, seemingly masking sadness. 'I've always been terrible at English. Reading books is enough of a challenge for me, never mind writing one, so I really need your help to get mine to a publishable standard. Prove something to myself.' He looks up at me through his long lashes, almost apologetically. There seems to be a weight to his words, his glance, and I'm acutely aware I feel an undeniable attraction to him.

'Well if you need me, I'm all yours,' I offer gaily, overcompensating. I'm both surprised and embarrassed by how brazen I sound, my cheeks flaming hot as I attempt to awkwardly backtrack. 'In a professional proofreading capacity, of course, I bluster, metaphorically kicking myself. Trust me to practically sabotage my own business before it's even got off the ground properly.

To my surprise he reaches over and touches me on the arm, smiling kindly. It's been a while since a man touched my skin directly. Despite his fingertips feeling warm and soft, I involuntarily flinch and look down at them, waiting for the grip to intensify, for the pressure to increase, but it doesn't. My heart rate does though, and not in a good way. 'I definitely need you,' he says, holding eye contact for a few seconds before withdrawing his hand.

'Great!' I say too brightly, huffing out a breath, standing to put on my coat, as businesslike as possible. I swallow, trying to keep the internal alarm at bay, to appear outwardly 'normal'. 'Well, email me the manuscript and I'll work through it and email the proofread version back to you within a couple of weeks for the price I quoted by email.'

'No rush,' he confirms, clearly a little startled by how swiftly I've wrapped up our meeting. 'It was great to meet you, Paige.' He stands too, to shake my hand again, grasping it for longer than necessary with a bemused expression on his face. I'm certain he must be able to feel my pulse vibrating through my wrist as the panic builds. I need to leave. Now.

I practically run to the safety of my car, grateful for the cool January drizzle then the familiarity of sitting behind the wheel. I focus on my breathing and wait for the fluttering, flapping wings in my chest to subside and for the pounding in my head to stop. It's been a year now; I thought these panic attacks had stopped for good.

Chapter Four

Continuing to face my social anxiety demons head-on, I've agreed to meet Joy in a new coffee shop in nearby Anlaby. I order a flat white for a change, choosing the skinny decaffeinated option. Since the surprise reoccurrence of a panic attack last week, I've decided to reduce my caffeine intake. Plus, working from home can expand your waistline if you're not careful, even with an active collie to walk, and I still remember the sting of past appearance-based insults all too sharply.

I collect my drink and carry it to the one remaining free table. Luckily for me, it is next to the large picture window so I can keep watch of passers-by and so Joy can spot me easily when she finally arrives. The small but cosy venue is quite busy as it's a Saturday morning and Joy is already late. Not that I mind as it gives me idle time to think about Aydan. I worked through the first few chapters of his book yesterday following our meeting on Thursday. Considering his dyslexia confession, he's clearly worked really hard on them, and they were a pleasure to proofread.

I smile at the memory of his self-deprecating attitude; in my experience it's rare to find a man like that. He didn't seem as put out as I'd assumed by my rushed departure either, messaging me afterwards to say how pleased he is that we're working together. The panic attack subsided much more quickly than they ever used to and I'm so relieved; the last thing I want to do is mess my life up again, especially when I'm on the cusp of creating a better one.

A swell of positivity takes me by surprise as I think back over the last few months, about everything I've achieved already, despite my difficulties. I need to actively try to remind myself that I'm doing well, all things considered, and to focus on the potential ahead for my business and my author career. I'm excited about working with Aydan on his book and starting the revision process on my own book, however challenging that may be.

I'm still battling with myself whether to ask the writing group for their opinion and advice on it though. They are so supportive and have given encouraging feedback on the few no-context snippets I have dared to share so far, but there are such diverse tastes and writing styles amongst us that I'm loath to ask any of them to be beta readers for the complete manuscript. Not only that but my soul is laid bare in those pages and even though it's written from my 'fictional' character's point of view, I'm not ready for anybody here to put two and two together about my shameful past just yet.

I sense a presence and look up to see Joy waving gaily at me from outside. I smile widely at her, as I usually do. Joy is the most cheerful and positive person I have ever met. However, she claims, in a very un-PC fashion, that she can "hold a grudge like a cursed gypsy" if anyone crosses her. Not that I've ever been on the receiving end, but she's openly shared enough of her stories with the writing group – many of which are based on real events, apparently – to make me fear ever getting on the wrong side of her.

Joy joined the group just a couple of weeks after me and we've struck up a good friendship and working relationship over the past months. Her tall tales certainly bring an element of fun to our weekly meetings, much to regimented Sylvie's chagrin, but she hasn't persuaded the rest of us to be as open when it comes to revealing aspects of our own personal lives yet. Ironically, we're mostly all closed books.

Joy has written three novellas so far, a series of erotic mysteries (which she describes as "a torrid coupling of *Fifty Shades* and *Midsomer Murders*"), which is still a massive achievement despite Sylvie's spiteful comment at last week's meeting. A dodgy vanity publishing house offered to publish them in exchange for a few thousand pounds, despite all three manuscripts still being riddled with spelling and punctuation errors after her own unsuccessful revision attempts. No in-house editing or proofreading was offered as part of the so-called deal. Poor Joy had been expecting a decent advance and a marketing budget, and her bubble was well and truly burst when she found out the publishing house wasn't reputable. 'Not meant to be!' she had proclaimed cheerfully, and is now considering submitting them elsewhere, or possibly following the self-publishing route.

And that's where I come in. I'm currently helping her to get them up to a submission standard – for mates' rates, which I'm keeping track of for when she can afford to actually pay me. It's quite an undertaking and way beyond my remit as a proofreader as they all contain gaping plot holes. I've been working on them for weeks already, but Joy is still stubbornly (yet extremely pleasantly) refusing any further professional intervention, against my repeated gentle advice. Thankfully our clashing opinions on her books haven't caused any damage to our friendship – yet.

A faux-fur-leopard-print-coat-clad Joy makes her way to the

table a few minutes later, sets her drink down and greets me with an air kiss on each cheek, as usual, always full of vim and vigour.

'Hello, darling, so delightful to see you,' she says, using the affectionate term she uses for everyone, like a theatrical luvvie. 'Now, I've had some more thoughts on the books...'

I laugh despite myself, used to the routine, pencil already poised over the dog-eared stack of manuscripts I've just retrieved from my bag. Joy's trilogy is the most farcical thing I have ever read – her split personality main characters are inconsistently abhorrent and the situations they either manufacture or find themselves in are frankly too far-fetched to be believable or even possible at times. There's suspension of disbelief and then there's the realm of complete craziness, yet she's insistent they remain outrageous, and truly believes there's a gap in the market for readers who crave pure wanton escapism.

I'm trying to make sure they're at least readable and we meet regularly to go over them. I should really be charging her more for my time, help and expertise but it doesn't seem right, not when we're in the same writing group. Never one not to learn from past mistakes, I'll know better next time not to offer my services for virtually free, especially as I want to build the business up sooner rather than later.

'Before we get into that though... Pray tell, what did I miss at group on Wednesday – anything exciting?' asks Joy, slipping her coat over her chair and stroking it like a beloved pet. 'You like?' She points to the coat proudly. 'It was a present from my son.'

Leopard print is not my taste at all, but I smile and nod politely. More interestingly, this is the first time Joy has mentioned her son and so I presume he was the reason why she didn't attend this week's meeting.

'Yes, actually, you did miss something,' I say, pleased to be able to tell her before Sylvie does. 'Belinda Penfold has offered us the chance to run a writing workshop at the Guildhall's book fair in March.'

'Belinda?' questions Joy, finally sitting down elegantly despite her calf-length red pencil skirt slightly restricting her movements. As I did with Aydan, I feel practically invisible in comparison in my old, cheap, nondescript clothing.

'Ultra-efficient event organiser... event planner... the very epitome of "together",' I say to describe Belinda. Joy still looks puzzled. 'Cross between Holly Golightly and a librarian... Kenny was intimidated by her at that poetry night in–'

'More intimidated than he is by Sylvie?' interjects Joy.

'Not possible,' I respond seriously. We're all quietly terrified of Sylvie. I make one last attempt to acquaint Joy with Belinda. 'She was the one wearing the Madonna headset, walking around with a clipboard.'

'Oh, yes, I remember her now!' exclaims Joy. 'She was shooing me and the very dapper gentleman I was speaking to out of a doorway because we were causing an escape hazard, allegedly.' She takes a sip of her coffee and licks the foam off her thin, bright-red lips. Her lipstick is smeared on just outside of her natural lip-line giving her a slightly Barbara Cartland air.

'Belinda takes her event planning responsibilities very seriously,' I state gravely. 'Anyway, she wants the book fair to appeal to a much more diverse audience than it usually attracts this year as we're the City of Culture, so she's bringing in community groups to teach classes as well as organising a few sellers' stalls to hopefully make it more of a full day out rather than a pop in.'

'And how was the workshop suggestion received at group?' asks Joy, arching one heavily pencilled eyebrow. I know what she's really asking: what did Sylvie think about it?

'I volunteered to help plan the workshop, which went down

well, especially as Lloyd did his usual woe-is-me routine. None of the others seemed that forthcoming except Renee, who said she would help on our book stall.'

'Poor old Lloyd... he really is hunkering down in those doldrums over his blasted books, isn't he? Truly mired in the past, bless him. Well, you can count on me being there as well, darling,' declares Joy. 'Could anyone else be persuaded to join in?'

'Well, according to an email Sylvie sent me afterwards, she is going to deliver the workshop herself now, so it looks like the rest of us will be supporting her.'

Joy makes a tsking sound and shakes her head although her back-combed helmet of hair doesn't move. 'That doesn't surprise me in the slightest... big limelight hogger!' she proclaims.

I laugh guiltily, more at Joy's tone of voice and turn of phrase than the insult behind it. Although I agree that Sylvie can be difficult at times, I'm not one for allegiances or cliques and I don't want Joy to consider me bitchy in any way. Although I'm still navigating being part of a group, I'm very aware of the effect of unkindness and nastiness and I don't want it bleeding into the present like a noxious gas.

'Anyway,' I say, changing the subject, 'let's get back to your thoughts on the books – which character's going to do what crazy thing now?'

Tell Me About Him

'So, tell me about him!' demanded Julia as she joined her in the staff canteen for lunch. 'I want proper details too, none of this glossing over the interesting bits.'

'Well,' she began, resting her elbows on the table and her hands under her chin, coyly pretending she hadn't been waiting eagerly for her new work friend and wasn't bursting with the need to tell her a few details about her new boyfriend, 'he's pretty great.'

Julia made a 'go on' motion with her hand while she took a bite of her deli-bought sandwich. Julia believed in indulging in little luxuries every day; she said that in her line of work as a journalist she saw enough depravity and pessimism.

She announced her prepared description. 'He's called Shane, he's from here – Leeds born and bred – and he's gorgeous!'

Julia simply stared at her while she swallowed. 'They're not details,' she said. 'They're basic facts – tell me things I wouldn't be able to glean or find out myself from talking to him for five minutes.'

She thought about it for a few seconds, frowning in concentration, deliberating how detailed to get. She considered Julia a good friend already, but she was wary about disclosing too much about Shane and besides, she wanted to preserve their private little bubble. She'd already got the impression he wouldn't like her gossiping to people about their relationship; he said he hated those types of women, the ones with no class or mystery about them.

Julia sensed her reluctance and sighed. 'Okay then, carry on glossing... what's his job at least?'

She looked down, feeling her cheeks heat slightly. Julia would notice; Julia noticed everything when she was getting the story, like an adept journalist should.

Julia did indeed notice her hesitation, and her embarrassment. 'Please tell me he's actually got a job,' she said, putting down her sandwich and rolling her eyes.

'He's looking for one...' she replied, defensive on his behalf. He'd be cross if he knew she had said anything; he was really sensitive about his unemployment status. 'He's thinking of starting his own business,' she added brightly, clutching for the positive. 'He's really into IT.'

'He's really into IT?' parroted Julia with a mocking laugh. 'That's just code for a work-shy tech geek who loves gaming.'

She looked down again, suddenly desperate to leave; she shouldn't have said anything. Julia picked up her sandwich again, studying her.

She stood, deliberately avoiding eye contact. 'Anyway, I'd better get back. See you later,' she said, collecting the remnants of her sparse, low-calorie lunch, and hurrying away.

— *Descent into Deceit*

Chapter Five

February 2017

I anxiously survey my tiny terrace whilst Hardy sits in his bed, clearly sensing my nervous energy. I've tidied and cleaned every inch of the living space, yet to my familiar eye it still looks drab and dingy. Despite moving in a whole year ago, the house has the same studenty feel and look about it as when I bought it. I wonder whether my paltry, budget-friendly attempts to inject colour and texture into the rooms have only succeeded in drawing even more attention to its shabby shell. At the time, it was one of the few houses for sale in my limited price range due to wanting to preserve the remainder of my inheritance for essential future living costs, and although Alliance Avenue certainly isn't the most salubrious street in Hull, it's near Westfield Park, which is perfect for walking Hardy.

I know I'm comparing my modest home unfavourably to Sylvie's stunning Georgian mansion-style house, but I can't help it; this is my first time hosting the writing group, my first time hosting anyone here. I've thought long and hard about whether to permit an invasion of my precious privacy, but I believe I've built up enough of a comfortable trust with the writing group by now, so I've decided to take the risk.

Glancing around again, I chew my bottom lip. Comparison is the thief of joy, I remind myself, yet still start slightly as the first knock sounds. Hardy barks once and jauntily leads the way out of the lounge diner to the narrow hallway, much more eager than me to receive our visitor.

It's Sylvie, of course, and she's holding her cafetière.

'Hello, Paige. Wednesday already! I've brought my own supplies, I can't stand instant,' she declares, waving the large coffee pot by way of a greeting as she steps over my threshold without waiting to be invited in. We stare at each other in my small hallway until I realise she wants me to take it off her and do something with it. 'I brought coffee and filters too,' she adds, rifling through her large designer bag while simultaneously trying to remove her coat, which I presume she wants me to take too, like a cloakroom attendant. Obligingly, I do.

'Well, this is... cosy.' Sylvie gives what she can see of the house a cursory, unimpressed glance and I feel even more ashamed of the drabness in the wake of her comment. 'Are we in here?' she asks pointlessly, already making her way through the only door to her right into the main living room. She settles herself down on my bargain yellow wing-backed chair in the small bay window, like an eccentric old aunt come to visit.

After hanging her coat up in the understairs cupboard, I pop my flushed face back within view. 'Coffee, then?' I enquire as I notice Hardy has parked himself down next to her. Traitor. She graces me with a smile and nods her assent as there's another knock at the door. I rush to open it, still proffering the cafetière.

'Ooh, proper coffees?' asks Kenny after our hellos. 'Sylvie's got a pot just like that.'

I squash myself against the wall to let him in.

'Yes, she hates instant,' adds Lloyd, squeezing in behind Kenny.

After herding them in with Sylvie, I shoot off to the

kitchen at the back of the house to make the drinks, muttering to myself under my breath, clattering spoons and mugs a bit more loudly than necessary so I don't overhear anything that might make me paranoid. My nervousness about people being in my house for the first time is already morphing into tetchiness.

A few minutes later, I'm about to carry the large coffee-laden tray through to the group when the door goes again. 'Could someone please get that?' I ask, concentrating on my cargo, terrified of my inherent clumsiness causing a cafetière catastrophe.

'Coo-ee!' calls a cheerful Joy as she and Renee enter my home while Kenny closes the door behind them. Renee sees me struggling through the kitchen doorway and rushes to my aid, plucking the coffee pot off the tray to ease my burden. As she does, I look over to navigate the route to my small dining table, conscious of Hardy being in the way as usual when he wants attention I see that Sylvie, Lloyd and Joy are already clustered around it. I frown, wondering what they are finding so interesting. Then I realise: my printed manuscript containing all the scribbled revision notes I've made so far is sitting right there for all to see.

I rush over with my tray of clattering mugs as they all shuffle away to make room for me. Sylvie deftly slides my manuscript aside and I notice the top few pages are skew-whiff and there's a guilty look on her face, if ever I saw one. They've been sneakily reading it. Fear snakes its way up my spine as I wonder how much they've got through.

'What the hell do you think you're doing?' I hear the panic in my raised voice followed quickly by Sylvie's sharp intake of breath at my never-used-before bad language. Joy and Lloyd exchange guilty glances but refuse to meet my glare.

Renee places the cafetière beside the tray of mugs and looks down at the table. 'Is this it, Paige?' She points to the pile of A4 paper. 'Is this your book? Can we have a read?'

At least she has bothered to ask permission – albeit after the other nosy parkers – but I'm too protective over it and its secret contents. If they read it there'll no doubt be questions I really don't want to answer yet, if ever. These people are the closest thing I have to friends – I think I can call them that now despite having very little frame of reference – and none of them are reading it until it's branded with a pen name, and I've worked out how to protect myself from its revelations. Getting it published is the goal; getting it published means I've got a better chance of staying in this new life I'm trying to create.

'Not yet, Renee,' I reply curtly. 'And I'll thank the rest of you to keep your nebby noses out in the meantime.' There's an awkward silence as I swipe it up and firmly deposit it on my desk in the corner, in front of the narrow window, the view to the side alley and backyard beyond as familiar to me as my own features due to the number of hours I have spent sitting there, lost in my terrible memories whilst writing the book.

I drop my shoulders, suddenly embarrassed about my out of character outburst and turn to face the room. 'I'm sorry,' I say. 'It's just... it's still a rough draft really. I need to finish revising it before I start submitting it to agents or publishers directly.'

'Submitting it?' asks Sylvie, frowning in confusion. 'You've never mentioned that before, Paige. I assumed you were planning to self-publish.' She returns to the yellow chair in the window as Kenny and Lloyd utilise the mismatched retro dining-table seats. I begin pouring the coffees.

'Well...' I begin, oscillating between staying annoyed with them and sharing my nervous excitement about my plans. I guiltily acknowledge that if the tables were turned, I would probably have sneaked a peek at one of their unpublished manuscripts too, especially if they had been as guarded about its contents as I have.

I start passing out the drinks – Sylvie's first – and decide to let them into my thought process, to be a bit more open for a change. 'I've been giving a couple of options some thought...' I begin as I hand the others their mugs too. Everyone murmurs their interest as I pull out a dining chair to sit on, all the comfy seats taken now that Joy and Renee are nestled on my small two-seater sofa. Hardy leaves Sylvie's side and comes to lie at my feet. I lean down to stroke him, pleased he's seen the error of his traitorous ways.

'But why bother, dear?' asks Sylvie, before I get a chance to say any more. 'Surely self-publishing is the way to go. It seems a waste of time to me. I mean, look what happened to poor Lloyd.' She sniffs, sits back and takes a sip of her coffee.

I shoot a look at Lloyd, worried he may have taken offence at Sylvie's comment but he just nods, staring at my threadbare carpet with a sad expression on his face.

'You're doing the right thing, darling,' chimes in Joy. 'But why not let one of us beta-read it for you before you send it off anywhere? I'm game – you're already helping me so it's only right that I help you too!'

'I'll happily beta-read it too, Paige,' Lloyd pipes up. 'I would refer you to my editor from back in the day, but I think she's moved on now and I doubt anyone at my old publishing house would take my calls anymore,' he adds, self-deprecating as always.

I stall for time. I'm anxious about accepting their offers, as kindly meant as they are. I'm writing under a pen name so using my writing group as beta readers would definitely affect that anonymity and it won't offer the professional feedback I crave, despite Lloyd securing a traditional publishing deal over a decade ago and effectively being the "expert" in the room.

Sylvie and Renee are self-published authors but their preferred genres and writing styles are so different to my own, that I worry they can't be objective enough either. Yet I'm still navigating trusting my own judgement and Sylvie's words are making me wobble. No, I must make a decision and stick to it, for once. I really think my book stands a chance of being traditionally published. It's a dream I've always secretly held, despite the self-publishing revolution, so I want to try and see what happens.

I take a deep breath. 'Thank you, everyone,' I say. 'But I've been thinking about this for a long time and I'm going to try my luck with the traditional route first – as soon as I've finished tinkering with it, of course.'

'Well, be prepared for heartache,' warns Sylvie, her bitter tone reflecting her own disappointment at being rejected countless times by countless publishers before she chose to self-publish. 'Remember, Joy was nearly ripped off, weren't you, Joy?'

Joy smiles graciously, hiding her own disappointment behind her usual cheery exterior. 'I certainly learned my lesson there!' she quips. 'I was so hopeful of getting one of those la-di-da book deals but alas, it was not meant to be. Yet self-publishing could be a possible route to riches nonetheless; my son – my number one fan, bless his heart – knows of lots of "indie" authors who are absolutely raking it in, and God knows I could do with a few extra pennies.' She blinks quickly a few times, her false lashes fluttering, while clasping the gold locket around her neck. It's the first time I've heard her sound even slightly sombre.

'Hear-hear,' adds Lloyd. 'More trouble than it's worth trying to traditionally publish, Paige. Publishers drop you like a hot potato as soon as your book sales begin to slow. Never again.' He shakes his head dejectedly.

'I'm definitely team self-publish too,' joins in Renee, raising a fist in the air in solidarity. 'It works for me, or rather worked for me – I'm currently clamouring for space on Lloyd's writer's block with him!'

Everyone chuckles, united in their experiences, resolute in their jaded wisdom.

I stay quiet, knowing full well how much I want to stick to my plan, despite the possible drawbacks. I don't want to risk languishing in a pre- or post-publishing abyss like Sylvie, Lloyd, Renee, Joy and Kenny, resigned to scrabbling around for the odd book sale, or a rip-off publishing deal. No, that's not for me – I want my story to be shared, albeit under a pen name, and I'm going to do it my way.

'Right then, enough chit-chat,' states Sylvie, delving into her bag and pulling out printed meeting agendas. 'Let's get down to business – the book fair is now just five weeks away!'

Nearly two hours later I breathe a sigh of relief as I close the door behind my fellow writing group members. I made it through hosting the meeting, including steering everyone away from the subject of my book and tolerating Sylvie's headmistress-esque bossiness, and now Hardy and I can close ourselves off from the world again. I need to recharge my introvert energy levels and Aydan's book awaits after lunch.

As I'm diligently proofreading a few more of Aydan's chapters, my vibrating phone makes me jump. I usually put it away in a drawer to avoid interruptions, not that I get many calls, messages or notifications due to not having an online presence, but I must have forgotten in my haste to get to work after losing the morning to the writing group meeting. It's an anonymous number and I accidentally press accept rather than decline;

something I never normally do, preferring to let voicemail do its job.

Tentatively, I bring the phone to my ear and I'm surprised to hear Aydan's voice greeting me. Since our initial meeting last Thursday, we've exchanged quite a few friendly emails and him saying my name feels strangely thrilling.

'Great timing. I'm working on your book right now,' I tell him after our initial hellos.

I know from his most recent email that he's working up north this week. Wherever he is now sounds windy and his voice sounds slightly muffled yet excited. 'That's great, Paige. Thanks so much but–'

The line crackles and I can't catch what he's saying. I tell him so.

'Hang on a second, I'll–'

The phone goes quiet for a few moments. Knowing he's a hands-on property developer, I imagine him standing inside the shell of a house he's either pulling apart or putting back together.

His voice returns in fragments. 'It's crazy... less than a week but... emails... like I know you so well already.'

The line is a bit clearer now, but I'm still only hearing snatches of sentences.

'...professional boundary but I want to... more than just help with the book... put it on hold... proper date with you... some free time?'

I'm stunned into silence, if I've filled in the gaps and interpreted what he said correctly, he wants to take me on a date?

'Why?' is all I can ask after a moment. The line crackles again but we're still connected.

'Why?' He laughs. 'Why wouldn't... out with you? You're amazing!'

I definitely heard that. I frown before glancing around my own house, waiting for the punchline, searching for the hidden camera filming the call and my reaction to his surprising proposition.

'Paige?' he queries, now clear as a bell. 'Are you still there? Please don't make me say all that again.' He chuckles softly and it's a delicious sound.

My immediate concern, surprisingly, is not for our professional working relationship. I'm too flattered and too attracted to him to mind postponing work on his book if it blurs boundaries. No, my concern is getting close to someone again, yet if I continue allowing my murky past to cloud my future, I'll never have a normal life, whatever that might look like. At least now I know what I *don't* want it to include.

Ignoring the negative devil whispering on my shoulder and allowing hope to override fear for once, I decide to take a chance on him. The worst has already happened as far as I'm concerned, and lightning rarely strikes twice.

'I'm still here and yes, I'd love to go on a date with you,' I reply.

Chapter Six

I'm in the middle of working through a particularly difficult chapter of my manuscript or trying to. I'm reopening old wounds, severing through scar tissue, and it's so painful. No rest for the wicked though, not even on a Sunday evening.

My phone vibrates, diverting my attention away from the whirling memories, and I'm thankful for the reprieve. I've been waiting to hear from Aydan, that he's arrived safely in Scotland.

> Arrived and checked in. Going out for a quick curry with the building crew soon – early start tomorrow. How's it going, AC? A xx

After he asked me out on Wednesday, we've continued texting and emailing like teenagers, sharing selected snippets of ourselves, playing *Would You Rather*, and telling stories by emojis alone. Despite his dyslexia, he has a great way with words, and emojis! I smile at the affectionate, abbreviated "Agatha Christie" refrain, which seems to have stuck since he first called me it. Despite not being a huge fan of nicknames (in my experience not all are well meant), I do take this one as a compliment.

Slightly deceptively, I report good progress with my book and tap out a smiley face and a thumbs up emoji. Even though I already like him a lot, it's far too soon to allow Aydan VIP access to my inner world.

> That's fantastic, Paige! Our date can be upgraded to an official celebration meal as soon as I'm back in Hull. My treat. A xxx

He has signed off with three kisses – one more than usual. I try not to read too much into it as it's still very early days, after all. Yet our relationship seems to have developed in one fluid movement, a gymnast's cartwheel, as though it's simply meant to be. Tutting, I warn myself about my inherent tendency towards serendipity – I've been terribly wrong before on that score – but I do want to allow myself to be tentatively hopeful about this one, after the horrors of the past. Could this really turn into something special?

I scroll back through all the messages and emails we've exchanged since I happily agreed to go on a date with him. In a very gentlemanly manner, he has explained that he would prefer to take things slowly, as if we're in tune somehow, as if he senses that's exactly what I need. Although I only have one other serious – and disastrous – relationship to compare it to, this fledgling one already feels good.

As though he knows how to reinforce my feelings, my phone vibrates with another text:

> Goodnight beautiful. A xxx

I reply with kisses of my own and cross the room to put my phone in a drawer out of reach, determined to concentrate on my book, however much I enjoy the distraction. These texts from Aydan have given me perspective though, and for that I'm grateful.

A second later, as I'm about to close the drawer of my battered vintage bureau, another message comes through. As wonderful as it is to be the subject of someone's attention, I don't want to feel overwhelmed. I frown then freeze as the message from an unknown number flashes up on my locked home screen, its one sentence visible:

> You can run but you can't hide…

I feel a painful scrunching sensation in my stomach and make it to the kitchen just in time to throw up into the sink. Hardy skitters around my ankles as I grip the countertop waiting for the shaking to subside. As I rinse my mouth, my head pounding, I again recite my usual reassurances:

It's not him. He doesn't know where you live. He's still locked up.

Which begs the obvious questions: If it wasn't him, who did send the text? And why?

The next morning, I'm walking Hardy with my headphones in, trying to listen to one of my motivational podcasts, to "top up my confidence well" but my brain continues to obsess over the anonymous message I received last night. My anxiety has ramped up, like a child on refined sugar, intent on destroying the positive pathways I've been forging in my brain, and trapping and trampling on the butterflies in my stomach that were beginning to thrive thanks to the writing group and Aydan.

The crisp air, usually a salving balm, is having no calming effect whatsoever and I walk with my head down around

Westfield Park's perimeter, hood up against the world, worrying and fretting even more than usual. I scold myself – I should know by now this is always the way: as soon as something good happens, something bad happens to counteract it. Or sometimes, something even worse happens like being struck by lightning after surviving a devastating earthquake.

I know I'm being dramatic, so I focus on considering the realistic possibilities, although they are few. The only people who have my new number are the writing group members and now Aydan. I think that's it. I don't even have my phone number on my basic, faceless website or business cards or flyers, preferring email contact only, and I don't have any social media profiles anymore, so nobody can contact me that way. Think, Paige, think. There's only one thing "running" could be referring to, but it can't be that. I've been careful. I moved miles away – twice. I changed my number. I created an anonymous business. I started again after shutting, bolting and barricading the door to the past.

Watching Hardy dart happily from one intriguing smell to the next, I suddenly feel a chill in my bones, and it's not because of the fresh February weather. With a jolt, I realise far too late: I didn't actually give Aydan my closely guarded phone number. So how the hell did he get it?

Chapter Seven

Waiting over a week for my first date with Aydan has been torturous in some ways and deliciously anticipatory in others. The text and email flirting has ramped up yet more notches in the interim, the physical distance between us only intensifying the excitement of the reunion to come, except this time there are no professional boundaries to be mindful of.

Still, despite Aydan's obvious eagerness, I'm consciously holding back. I still don't know how he got my phone number and that's something I need to broach tonight as casually as possible, without revealing why I'm so protective about it. I'm also still living on my nerves after the anonymous message last Sunday, and I still have no clue who sent it. I feel like I've moved through the week in a trance. Despite attempting to act normally at the writing group on Wednesday, Sylvie's shrewd comment about me being there "in body but not in spirit" confirmed otherwise.

Despite the chilly evening, Aydan is waiting outside the newly opened fancy-looking restaurant overlooking the marina when I arrive. A cavalcade of internal butterflies are flapping their wings wildly, reminding me that my excitement is currently overriding my reservations about getting involved with anyone again. How easily my supposed reluctant heart changed tack, but I must admit, these past few days flirting with Aydan have felt so good. Due to him working away during the week, he only has Friday evenings and Saturdays free, and although we've technically only known each other just over two weeks, the concertinaed courtship of sorts has escalated rapidly despite his initial suggestion about taking things slowly.

He is on his phone, head down, talking quietly to someone as I approach. He glances up, spots me and ends the call immediately. I appreciate the courtesy and the fluttering intensifies as I realise I am about to spend an entire evening being his centre of attention. I'm severely out of practice on the dating front though; it's been over three years since I last went out with anyone.

I reach him, unsure about how to greet him, suddenly ridiculously nervous. Surprisingly, he takes the initiative and kisses me directly on the mouth – with enough pressure to let me know how he feels about me without giving the people in the bar area on the other side of the double glass doors a seedy show. It's lovely but the instant intimacy throws me off and I break away and take a step back. If he notices he doesn't mention it.

'Ready?' he asks with an easy smile. I nod whilst simultaneously admonishing myself for being so affected by a man I'm attracted to wanting to kiss me.

Inside, the maître d' leads us to a cosy table for two in the corner of the dining area, as per Aydan's request. I'm touched that he remembered my preference for being tucked away rather than in the limelight. I gaze around in appreciation as my anxiety starts to dissipate, and my worries about the mystery message edge further into the background. I want to enjoy tonight if I can. The restaurant is lovely and very posh – polished wood and cream leather seating, panelled walls and beautiful chandeliers punctuating the high, dark ceilings. Very art deco and very much my style.

I take off my coat to reveal my favourite floral midi dress, worn in an effort to override Aydan's memory of the plain black jeans and shirt I wore when we met. His gaze lands on me appreciatively and I feel myself flush.

'Wow,' he says as he pulls out my seat for me. 'You look beautiful, Paige.' I'm pleased he approves. 'Sorry about the shabby surroundings,' he jokes from across the table as he sits down. 'Everywhere else was booked.' He grins at me the same way he did at our first meeting, quietly confident that I would be impressed. I am, on all counts.

'It'll do I suppose.' I sigh playfully, my eyes flitting from the beautiful abstract prints on the walls to the mouth-watering dessert trolley, to the other diners in their glad rags too. A handsome man wearing an expensive-looking striped shirt catches my eye at the very same moment I catch his. I look away quickly, embarrassed, back to Aydan, who is watching me, smiling. Our gazes lock and that one look tells me exactly what he's hoping for later. I feel the heat burst onto my cheeks again, instantly as hot as the flaming pans in the exposed kitchen area to my left.

'Aydan?' A man appears at our table, holding out his hand for Aydan to shake. It's the same man who just caught me looking at him, and he knows Aydan!

'James! How're you doing, mate?' exclaims Aydan, clearly pleased to see him. As they exchange animated greetings, I smile shyly at the floor, waiting for Aydan to introduce us, and he soon does. 'James, this is Paige, my girlfriend.' My eyes widen fractionally, surprised at the term. We've certainly never discussed our brand-new relationship status before this – our very first date. 'Paige, this is James Locksley,' he says.

I recover quickly and hold out my hand to James too, which he takes I feel a jolt of electricity zap through me and gasp, taken completely off guard. James is categorically not my type. He's rugged and stocky and overtly manly – strong hands and a shaved head. His smile reveals a slightly chipped front tooth, which only adds to his attractiveness. He's the complete opposite of hipster Aydan, who is definitely my type, yet I feel strangely self-conscious in James's presence and just nod a shy hello.

'Anyway, I'm sorry to interrupt,' says James as Aydan sits back down. 'I'll leave you to it, I just wanted to say hello... oh, how's your book coming?'

Aydan looks across the table at me and grins. 'Shelved for now, mate. Can't compete with yours anyway.'

James smiles at the compliment. 'Nonsense,' he says. 'Plenty of room for everyone when it comes to publishing.'

'Well I've got other priorities at the moment... work and whatnot,' explains Aydan. He winks at me, and I feel a jolt of pleasure.

James glances at me and nods, clearly understanding Aydan's not so subtle comment. 'I remember the struggle well. Enjoy your evening – lovely to meet you, Paige.'

He returns to his own table and two male companions, right in my eyeline, and I am hyper aware of him in my peripheral vision.

'Has James written a book too?' I ask Aydan, who is studying the drinks menu.

Aydan nods. 'He wrote a property investment book too, a couple of years ago. Published it himself. It did quite well actually – apparently being an indie author can be big business. Now, what do you say to a bottle of champers for starters, AC?'

'Champagne? For starters? What's for afters?' I tease, bravely for me, carried away with the occasion and Aydan's generosity and buoyancy.

'Wait and see.' Aydan smiles broadly, signalling for the waiter.

Later, as the taxi drops us back at my house, there's no question about Aydan – my boyfriend, apparently – coming inside, the idea of taking things slowly completely forgotten. After a few glasses of champagne and three courses of intense flirting, we were barely able to keep our hands off each other during the fifteen-minute taxi journey back to mine, and it was only as we were travelling past Westfield Park and almost home that I realised I'd forgotten to ask how he had my phone number in the first place. But the thought left my head as Aydan's fingers moved further and further up my inside thigh.

No sooner are we through the front door, I let him kiss me hungrily, practically pawing at me with desire, while Hardy fusses around our feet, impatient for my attention. It feels like we're long-lost lovers finally reunited after years of separation, not just mere weeks apart. It feels good to be touched by him, taken by him for the first time, albeit a bit rougher than I prefer.

Is that why, as soon as Aydan is in my bed asleep, in a state of tipsy bliss, I find myself googling James Locksley?

Chapter Eight

Hardy jaunts happily ahead of me around Westfield Park. It's Tuesday teatime and the familiar green space is relatively quiet, just how I prefer it. As I round the corner of the wide footpath surrounding the centre of the park, I spot the most beautiful copper-coloured red setter bounding over the large expanse of grass, off its lead and loving life, its owner striding behind it, futilely trying to close the distance between them, framed by the impending mid-February early sunset.

I smile at the scene despite Hardy's attempts to tug my shoulder out of its socket in his desperation to reach this mysterious canine stranger, and I try to steer him away to the other side of the path. He's always eager to meet other dogs but I don't fancy having to make polite conversation with a fellow owner today, not when I've got so much work to continue as soon as we get home. I normally leave it until later in the day for his second walk, preferring to be obscured by the dusk, but as I feel like I'm wading through mud with my book revisions, I grabbed his lead and headed out of the house, desperate for fresh air and to get out of my own head for a while.

I'm struggling to stay in the present as I work steadily

through my wretched memories, unearthing difficult and complicated feelings yet again. I've barely achieved anything so far this week, so this is my attempt to reset my brain as well as get my steps in; having as much control over my weight as I do the rest of my life is still a renewed thrill these days.

Not that Aydan had any complaints whatsoever about my waistline, or any other part of my body for that matter, on Friday night after our first official date at the restaurant. I feel my face heat at the flashback and acknowledge that my fiery blush is as much due to what I did afterwards than what I did with Aydan. I'm embarrassed to admit I've become a bit of an internet stalker where James Locksley is concerned, telling myself I'm only interested in his author profile whenever the guilt starts to nip at me.

'Red!' I hear someone shout, followed by a whistle. I turn and see the red setter making its way towards us at speed, furry face open and expecting an affectionate greeting in return after no doubt hundreds of previous encounters resulted in such an outcome. Who wouldn't want to fuss such a beautiful dog?

I relent and let Hardy's lead slacken as the two dogs greet each other, sniffing and jostling playfully. It's a lovely sight and I don't realise the red setter's owner has reached us until I look up and come face to face with none other than James Locksley. What are the odds? My cheeks instantly flame again, and I struggle to compose myself for a moment. He looks windswept and healthy and happy, and he's got a gorgeous dog. Quite the combination.

I remove my headphones and stuff them in my pocket, along with my hands, attempting to look casually prepared for a conversation with a stranger that I currently probably know more about than my own boyfriend.

'Sorry about her.' He laughs. 'She's more whippet than setter when she wants to be.'

I smile and then watch the penny drop as he recognises me.

'It's Paige, isn't it?'

I'm flattered he's remembered my name. 'Yes, hi... James, right?' I pretend that I don't know his full name is James Lawrence Locksley as I unclip Hardy and allow him more freedom to play. He barks his excitement and zooms off, enticing Red to follow.

'That's right.' James leans in to kiss my cheek, cupping my elbow, the physical touch taking me by surprise and causing a pleasurable jolt. 'How was your night out on Friday? Great food, wasn't it?'

I blink several times, momentarily blindsided by him being in such close proximity, my senses on overdrive. He smells so good. An image of Aydan flashes in my mind and I instantly shake it away. Boldly and quite out of character, I can't help indulging in a little attention-seeking behaviour in order to forge common ground.

'Delicious. It was definitely a fitting celebration,' I dangle, hoping he's going to ask me to elaborate.

'Celebration?' he enquires.

'Yes, I've just finished writing my first novel, so Aydan took me out as a bit of a well done.'

'Wow,' he says, seeming genuinely thrilled for me. 'Well done indeed!'

'Thank you.' I blush again, suddenly embarrassed about bragging, despite orchestrating the compliment. 'Aydan said you've written a book too, haven't you?' I ask, desperate to fling the limelight over to him.

'I did, yes,' he says, rocking back on his heels, blue eyes twinkling from beneath his flat cap, lips hinting at a smile. 'Nearly three years ago now though.'

'That's fantastic!' I match the enthusiasm he showed about my achievement. 'What was it about?' I ask, despite already knowing the answer from my internet foraging. I watch Hardy and Red chase each other in ever increasing circles in between stealing glances at him, too shy to meet his seemingly interested gaze.

'Boring property investment stuff. *Put Your Money Where Your House Is.*' He laughs as he reveals the title, which I already know, and really like. 'Nothing exciting, but it did okay,' he says modestly. 'I'm not clever enough to write novels like you.'

The self-deprecating comment reminds me of Aydan, and Lloyd with his woe-is-me failed author "banter", except James doesn't sound very woe-is-me. He sounds very confident and assured of himself, which makes me realise he's paying me a compliment.

A bark interrupts the moment, and I'm pleased to have a reason to focus my attention elsewhere. Hardy appears at my side, tongue lolling, and flops down next to me, all ran out. I laugh at the cuteness of him. James clicks his fingers and Red bustles up next to him too.

'So how exactly do you know Aydan then?' I ask. 'He didn't say.'

'We met at the end of last summer – just the once – at a property auction in Leeds. We got chatting after bidding on the same lot. He seemed a good bloke. Bit of a coincidence seeing him here in Hull. Does he live here now?'

I simply nod and smile, feeling suddenly awkward about discussing Aydan with James, especially as I don't actually know whether my own boyfriend does lives here permanently or not. 'Well, I'd better get this one home for his afternoon snooze. Lovely to see you again, James,' I say, clipping Hardy's lead back on his harness. Despite enjoying being in his presence, I want to leave before he can ask any more questions about Aydan that I won't know the answers to and before I somehow manage to say something ridiculous or embarrassing, or both.

'Oh Paige, are you going to the book fair next month at The Guildhall?' he slips in, just as I begin to walk away.

I stop in my tracks and look back at him as a zap of excitement pinballs through me – I know in that instant that he's going too. I volunteer my information all too readily. 'Yes, my writing group is teaching a class in the adjoining hall, as well as running a stall.'

'I'll look forward to seeing you there then.' He smiles warmly and holds my gaze for a few seconds as my stomach flips. Am I imagining this spark between us?

He turns then heads off in the opposite direction, taking long, strong strides across the field, Red still unleashed and bounding by his side obediently, quite contrary to her earlier whippet antics.

As I wait for my heart rate to return to its usual rhythm, I stare after him, probably not dissimilar to the way Hardy looks at me when he wants a treat, and I realise I'm already in trouble.

She Said Yes

Friday night in, alone, together. Absolute perfection. They always scoffed at those "date night" couples, those who needed the excuse, the crutch for their relationship. Not them, though. DVD boxsets and takeaway pizza were the only guests allowed within their smug bubble of happiness, granted VIP access within. They would lay on the battered leather sofa, bathed in candlelight, wrapped around each other like sloths, only moving to reach for another slice of pepperoni, or each other's body parts. They often had to rewind episodes to catch up on what they had missed during their passionate interludes, which were frequent in those days. The snoozing puppy completed their happiness.

The proposal came after three months. On bended knee, in his house, which was not actually his house as it turned out, but she had begun to think of it as home, as her favourite place to be, with him. She gleefully messaged her friend Julia a picture of her ring, justification for all those missed coffee dates and ignored catch-up requests. It was crazy, looking back. How well can two people really know each other in three months? Yet she said yes, unreservedly, her internal timeline ticking the engagement and marriage boxes with pleasure, right on track.

Except the track was rotten, infected, veering towards an as yet invisible cliff in the distance, at speed.

— *Descent into Deceit*

Chapter Nine

I arrive home from the park, feed Hardy and check my emails. I'm surprised to find a flurry of them and quickly scan each one.

Lloyd: Hi, Paige. I'd like to talk to you about something. Can you meet me either before or after the meeting tomorrow? Thanks.

Joy: Darling! I think I've figured out how to fill that cavernous plot hole you pointed out in book three. How about Master Hamilton's secret lover turns out to be a double-crossing pilot and charters one of his private jets to New Zealand as an escape mission? Too much, or can I make it work?

Sylvie: We may have two new writing group members — one definite and one to be confirmed. The definite I met at my WI coffee morning yesterday. Not a published author per se but trying to be (I've warned her about the pitfalls — ha!). She says she's going to attend the next meeting. It's at Kenny's house, isn't it? Please confirm, Kenny.

Kenny: Yes, my house for tomorrow's meeting. See you all there (excuse the mess).

Sylvie: Update from Belinda. We need to be at the book fair by 9am on the day to start setting up the stall and the writing workshop. We will go over everything in more detail as soon as introductions for the group's new members are out of the way.

Reading through the messages, I note the mention of new writing group members with interest and briefly consider how they will change the group dynamic, because it's inevitable that they will. Hopefully for the better. The group feels a bit stagnant right now, as though people are resistant to change and new ideas, and that concerns me. As someone who has wholeheartedly embraced dramatic changes more than once, I'm not one for putting up and shutting up. Not anymore. There is also a slightly bitter undertone developing towards Sylvie and I wonder how long allowances will continue to be made for her before a potential mutiny occurs.

It makes me so sad; joining the writing group a few months after moving here gave me something new and mentally uplifting to focus on, something to mark each new week as another week survived, as well as another week establishing my new life and celebrating leaving my old one behind. Without knowing it, the group gave me the confidence to finally finish writing my story and to come to terms with what had happened to me, as a way to exorcise my demons and design a better future. I'm grateful to them for igniting that spark in me and I would hate for the meetings to become unenjoyable.

I transfer Sylvie's message thread to my writing group email folder and after a bit of deliberation, confirm with Lloyd that I can meet him before tomorrow's meeting. Aside from Joy, I haven't spoken to anyone else in the group on a one-to-one basis and although it's an intriguing request, it does make me nervous too. What on earth could he need to speak to me about? I just hope he's not just angling for a private confidence boost or to moan about Sylvie because I'm not the right person for either of those. I'm not so easily manipulated anymore.

There's also a new text from Aydan. I still haven't asked him how he got my number in the first place, and I don't feel as though I can now, not when we've been intimate. The very fact I slept with him suggests I trust him, so I don't want to offend him by quizzing him when the reason for doing so was to ask me out. I did google it and apparently there's a way to find out someone's phone number if you have their email address, so that must have been how he did it. It's flattering he wanted to surprise me, actually.

The time stamp on this message tells me it came through while I was talking to James in the park, and I feel another pang of guilt that I didn't even think to check my phone while walking home. I wasn't thinking about Aydan at all.

> Plumbing problems at the Scotland property –
> no chance of getting home this weekend.
> Missing you. Can't wait to see you next
> weekend though. I might even do that thing
> you said you liked again. ;-) A xx

As I always do after checking my messages lately, I breathe a sigh of relief that there are no new anonymous ones. There haven't been any more as yet, but that doesn't mean there won't be. It's infuriatingly frustrating not knowing if it's something I should be seriously worried about or not. *You can run but you can't hide*... implies being chased or caught but the only person that could possibly relate to is safely behind bars in a different city. No, it must have been a wrongly sent text; perhaps even a really bad joke meant for someone else. I want to believe that so badly.

I reply to Aydan with two miserable-face emojis and one blush-face emoji. I'm ignoring the fact I don't feel more disappointed about him having to work this weekend. I tell myself it's a defence mechanism – not getting too close to someone new – but surely I shouldn't be fantasising about another man so soon into a brand-new relationship, however tempting he seems on paper?

I shake my head to reset my thoughts, make myself a cuppa and return to my desk to continue revising my book, feeling a lot more refreshed and ready to focus. I'm nearly a quarter of the way through this hard copy first edit now and the pencilled notes crammed in margins, proofreading marks littering the text and scribbled questions at the foot of pages are my way of forcing myself to consider this novel as objectively as possible, as a reader would.

A pleasing burst of optimism blooms within me and I realise I'm starting to trust my own instincts again, after regretting so many bad choices and decisions for so long. Doing this myself is a necessary part of the process and the satisfaction I'll feel once my novel is finally finished will be worth it. Presenting the best version of my book to a publisher or agent will ensure it stands a better chance than simply submitting it and hoping for the best, like Joy did. No, I need to learn from the writing group's and my own past mistakes if I'm really going to make my new life, and this novel, a success. This time will be different, I'll make sure of it.

Chapter Ten

Lloyd is already hovering on the pavement outside Kenny's pleasant semi-detached home near the centre of Cottingham when I arrive on Wednesday morning. He looks anxious and a bit wired, which is unusual for the usually laid-back, demotivated Lloyd.

He waves, walking over to my car and holding my door open unnecessarily, obviously eager to speak. 'Thanks for coming early, Paige. There's a small park across the road – we could just pop over there for our chat?'

I nod, my own anxiety rising as I lock the car and follow Lloyd to a dewy, wooden bench. As I perch on the edge, he pulls a thick wad of paper from his bag without preamble.

'What's this?' I ask, frowning, suddenly worried. He has the air of a man with something important to share. Is it hard evidence against me? What has he found out?

'It's my new book. I've finally finished it. It's only taken me six years!' he explains excitedly, waving the manuscript in front of my face before sitting down next to me.

'Wow, Lloyd. Congratulations!' I reply with relief, genuinely pleased for him. He's been stuck in such a funk about his books, but I see now he's been hiding this secret and throwing us all off even suspecting that he's been working on something new. Seems like I'm not the only guarded group member, after all.

'Will you proofread it for me, Paige? Being a novel, it's a complete diversion from my previously published textbooks and I'd greatly appreciate your professional eye.' He fixes me with a desperate stare, clearly willing me to say yes, like a child begging for permission to stay up past their bedtime. I observe how nervous he is, how much this means to him, and suddenly I'm terrified to agree, unsure of my own capabilities. So much rests on this for him – his confidence, his reputation, his livelihood. I know he yearns to make money from writing again.

'Thank you so much for considering me, but are you sure? I've only been in business a few months; wouldn't you rather ask one of your old publishing contacts?'

'No chance,' he practically spits. 'If this turns out to be a dud too, I'll never live it down. I know you'll be kind, even if it is rubbish.'

He watches me closely, obviously sensing my hesitation. He tuts softly. 'Come on, Paige, we're in the same boat now, you and me, we've both just finished our manuscripts and we can do each other a favour.'

'A favour? What do you mean?' I ask, a prickling feeling nipping the back of my neck, a memory rattling the handle of a closed drawer in my mind. Being asked for favours has never ended well for me.

'You proofread my book for me, and I'll reach out to one of my old contacts to take a look at your book in exchange. It could be a foot in the door for you.'

'I thought you said you didn't have any sway with your old publishing contacts?' I ask, eyebrows raised.

'Yes, well, what I say and what I do are two different things.

Do you really think I want to announce to the group that I'm still "in" with a few useful people? They'll be pestering me to pass on their writing tripe. You've read Joy's books – as fun as she is, I'm not sabotaging what little reputation I might have left putting in a good word for that dross. They're all desperate to be successful writers but they're all talk, no action and very little talent. Happy to complain about their supposed hard luck instead of trying to change it. I just joined in all this time.'

I'm too shocked to speak for a moment. This is a version of Lloyd I have never seen before. Suddenly he seems to have an edge and I'm not sure whether my goosebumps are due to his cold attitude or the damp February air.

I find my voice again. 'So why do you stay in the writing group?'

'I was going to leave a few months ago but then you joined, and you were like a breath of fresh air into that stale environment. I could tell your writing had potential straight away, what little you did share, and you were so enthusiastic about the writing process and so interested in the rest of us and our experiences... I knew it would only be a matter of time until you finished your book. You're a doer, Paige, unlike the rest of them. I daren't risk letting my old contacts read my book yet, but I can pass yours on. And I do value you as a fellow author – I want to help you, if you'll help me in return.' He smiles as the top few pages of his manuscript flutter in the breeze. He slaps his palm down on top of them.

I relax slightly as I realise he doesn't have any sinister motives after all; he is just a beaten-down writer trying to get himself back on track. I berate myself for my suspicious assumption; not everyone always has ulterior motives.

'So, if I proofread your book and effectively give it my seal of approval, it'll give you the confidence to publish it yourself?' I ask.

'Yes, albeit under a pen name, like you. If it turns out to be a bestseller, I'll "out" myself as the author, but I'm still a bit wary. It's not my usual style; it's genre fiction so it's new territory for me.'

I observe his eager and hopeful expression. Despite his bitterness about the publishing industry, this is the most animated I've ever seen Lloyd and I understand why he wanted to talk to me alone. If the writing group find out he's written another book they'll be desperate to have a look, just as they were desperate to have a nosy at mine, to judge whether he's a better writer and has the potential to be more successful than them, particularly Sylvie. Despite Lloyd being one of the cheeky culprits at my house, maybe he was just checking my book was worth passing on to his contact. I feel quite honoured, although the thought of an agent or editor seeing it before it's ready makes me feel a bit queasy.

'Okay, I'll proofread it for you, but there's no need for an instant favour in return, I'm still a way off finishing my revisions.' I take Lloyd's manuscript from him and stow it in my bag.

'Thanks, Paige, I really appreciate it.' He sighs heavily, seemingly relieved and pleased in equal measure. 'Whenever you're ready, I'll forward your book on,' he offers as we begin walking back towards Kenny's house.

'I want to go through the whole thing again carefully before I even think about that,' I reply. 'Bit of a personal learning curve... but thank you.'

'No problem, and thanks again, Paige.' He grins and taps his nose. 'Not a word to the others, remember?'

As we approach Kenny's door. I pluck up the courage to state my proofreading fee. The promise of a "favour" won't keep my business afloat.

'Oh,' says Lloyd, visibly put out. 'I thought I'd get the same concession as Joy – you're doing hers for mates' rates, aren't you?'

I squirm. I had hoped he didn't know that, but people do talk, don't they? I need to be braver – I can't take on more work at a discounted rate, especially now that Aydan isn't a paying client anymore.

'I'm not *doing* her books,' I lie. 'I'm just acting as a sounding board; you know how crazy her plots are. She needs a bit of realism in the mix, that's all. What I've quoted you *is* mates' rates for a full manuscript proofread. The industry guidelines are more than that. I'm happy to email you proof if you need it.' I hope he can't detect the slight tremor in my voice as I state my case as confidently as I can.

'All right, I'll agree to your price for the first ten chapters. Then we can negotiate.' He winks. 'No rush though, I know you're busy with your book. And you can say that again about Joy's plotlines – that woman has the most outrageous imagination I've ever heard!' He shakes his head as he chuckles.

I frown at his implied assumption of a later discount – which I won't be agreeing to – but before I can muster up more courage to put him straight, Kenny opens the door and welcomes us in from the cold, Lloyd's secret manuscript stowed safely in my bag.

Chapter Eleven

Kenny shows us through to his small but cosy living room and bustles back to the kitchen to make the drinks – the cafetière seems to be making the rounds. Sylvie, early as usual, has already parked herself in the only armchair so Lloyd and I take the settee. Renee and Joy are yet to arrive but when they do, it's going to be a squash fitting us all in.

Kenny's house feels very seventies – mismatched, heavily patterned furnishings and carpets and teak furniture that's seen better days (not unlike my own shabby furniture I note honestly). There are stacks of books on every surface and newspapers open at almost completed crosswords, adorned with coffee stains and biro notes, and a dust covering you can write your name in on the TV screen. He did warn us about the mess.

Sylvie is barely disguising her look of disgust and I can see she wishes she'd brought her own china cup too as Kenny returns with chipped mugs of coffee for us all. He deposits each of them on top of the various books and newspapers within our reach, and as another knock sounds, he rushes off to answer the door.

Whilst he's out of the room I follow Sylvie's sour gaze

around Kenny's personal effects, marvelling at how she gets away with being so judgemental. I spot a black and white photograph on the cluttered mantelpiece and get up to have a look. They're a handsome couple – the man and woman in the picture. He's wearing a full police uniform and she's beaming up at him with obvious pride, her arm linked proprietorially through his. The glass is so dirty it's blurring the image, but I wonder who the young policeman is in relation to Kenny – father or brother perhaps? I don't comment on it or show it to Sylvie or Lloyd, especially after I chastised them for being nosy at my house.

Renee and Joy enter the room amidst a chorus of apologies for being late and I dart back to my seat on the sofa before I get usurped from the spot.

A moment later Kenny brings in two tall barstools for additional seating. 'I've no other comfy chairs,' he explains, embarrassed, as Sylvie's face contorts unattractively.

Renee squeezes on the settee between me and Lloyd, at Joy and Kenny's insistence, while they perch, quite happily, on the stools.

Sylvie, eager for the meeting to begin, and no doubt end, distributes the agenda. Number one, as expected, is the book fair, which is now just over three weeks away.

'As I shared in my recent email,' she starts, 'Belinda has confirmed the details of the book fair timings. We need to be there by 9am to start setting up the stall and–'

The doorbell interrupts Sylvie's update. We look around at each other, all present and correct, confused for a moment.

'Oh! The new members!' Sylvie exclaims. 'Well, don't keep them waiting, Kenny.'

As Kenny dutifully hops down off his stool to answer the door, Joy and I exchange a look, aghast at Sylvie bossing him about in his own home.

Kenny returns with a smart-looking lady, in both style and presence. She's older than me but definitely within the average age of the group, who are all in their fifties or sixties.

Sylvie surprises us all by jumping up to greet our guest with two air kisses, like a long-lost friend. 'Welcome, Madeleine!' she cries, without a hint of disdain, as Kenny disappears to presumably procure yet another stool. I hope he has enough. Nobody else arrives but Sylvie doesn't appear to have noticed yet, so enthralled is she with this new member.

We all greet Madeleine warmly from our seats, with only Joy matching Sylvie's uber enthusiasm, as is her way, and offering up her stool. Madeleine takes it, thanking Joy, as Kenny returns with a fold-up plastic garden chair and positions it in the only remaining space, just in front of the living-room door. It may be unconventional but we're all in and I feel strangely affectionate towards Kenny and his quiet, contented, make-do attitude.

'Now, I was updating everyone about our upcoming book fair, but shall we do formal introductions instead, for Madeleine?' asks Sylvie.

We all agree as it wasn't really a question. Sylvie begins, of course, in her element centre stage.

'Well, hello and welcome, Madeleine,' she repeats. 'As you know, I formed this writing group a few years ago now – it began with just myself and Renee and has grown steadily to include everyone here, with some others falling by the wayside, as is often the case with differing personalities.' She sniffs, smiles tightly and continues. 'I started the group when I began writing my first fairy-tale fantasy novel, which has since been published, as a way to connect with fellow local writers. Despite the success of this little group, in that we meet regularly and offer each other support, I had hoped that my book would do much better than it has. Although, saying that, I am absolutely hopeless at marketing the damn thing! I'm going to be much more on the ball with book two.'

It's the most reflective I've ever heard Sylvie sound – usually the authority on all things writing related – and I feel a slight pang of pity for her. I can only imagine how crushing it must be to devote so much time and energy into writing your book for it to be less successful than you hoped. I'm surprised to hear that Sylvie is either considering, or already working on, a second book too as this is the first time she's mentioned it. I'm not the only one to pick up on this – Joy comments immediately.

'Book two? Since when, Sylvie? You never said, you dark horse!'

'Yes, well, I've had an idea and written the first chapter but that's all I'm going to say on the matter,' she replies, seemingly hesitant to speak, for once.

'Good for you, Sylvie,' adds Lloyd and I wonder whether he might feel like sharing his own news, but he remains tight-lipped by my side.

Everyone nervously glances at each other, unsure whether Sylvie is going to select who will introduce themselves next or whether we should just jump in. To abate the awkwardness, I go next.

'Hi, Madeleine,' I begin, raising my hand in a pointless half wave. 'I'm Paige and it's lovely to have you here – we haven't had a new member since I joined the group last August. I finished my first novel a few weeks ago and I'm now in the process of revising it. I'm a freelance proofreader by profession, so it's all a bit of a busman's holiday for me. I'm really hoping to be published one day, although whether that's traditionally or self-published, I've yet to decide!'

Madeleine smiles encouragingly at me before her eyes move over to Lloyd who has just cleared his throat and moved forward on the viciously patterned settee in preparation for his turn.

'Lloyd,' he says, also splaying his hand in greeting. 'I had a traditional publishing deal about ten years ago for two non-fiction textbooks, the first of which did pretty well thanks to some big orders from schools all around the UK. Nothing even remotely successful since though, so I need to get my finger out sharpish! I'm considering writing a novel next as soon as inspiration strikes!' He glances sideways at me before sitting back with a nod to punctuate the fact he's done. I don't say a word; it's not my news to share.

Next in the circle is Renee. 'Hello, Madeleine. I'm Renee and I've self-published three stand-alone children's books so far. The last one was about seven years ago now. They all sold well thanks to the school and library visit circuit, which I loved doing. However, since going back to work part time to help my son out with his university fees after my husband was made redundant, I just don't have the time or energy for that level of promotion anymore. It's a shame but family comes first,' she states, definitely not sounding like she means it. She looks down to pick an invisible thread off her trousers, a frown on her face.

The atmosphere shifts in the wake of Renee's introduction and I sense her frustration. Although we conducted introductions when I joined, she didn't mention anything about her family and financial struggles then. There must be something in the air today prompting either secrets or sharing.

Only Kenny and Joy remain.

'Shall I go next, my love?' Joy asks Kenny and he politely gestures for her to do so.

'Madeleine, what a beautiful name!' she tinkles brightly. 'I'm Joy McLellan and I'm a writer of erotic romance fiction. Three books written so far – a series if you will – yet not a sniff of a proper publishing deal, and believe me, I have tried! I thought after the success of that *Fifty Shades* I'd be quids in, but apparently not! Too late to the party, I think, which is most unlike me!' I smile at Joy's honesty, as does everyone else as I glance around the room.

Madeleine seems comfortable and makes interested noises and brief comments, despite all the new information flying at her from all directions. I wish I could project that level of confidence in social settings.

We all look expectantly at Kenny.

'I'm Kenny Law,' he states quietly, in his unassuming manner. 'I've always written, since being a young boy, and I like writing poems and short stories mainly. I've tried to write a book a couple of times, but I just can't seem to get the momentum going. I joined the group in the hope that their motivation will eventually rub off on me so I can make something of myself in my retirement. I'm not used to not being productive.'

Our collective voices clamour to bolster Kenny about his writing skills and I'm struck by how many deflated dreams there are in the group, how sad it is that these people who love writing so much (perhaps with the exception of Joy who openly admits she's trying to cash in on an already successful franchise) also suffer so much disappointment at the hands of it. It makes me all the more determined to get my book out there and do whatever it takes to help make it a hit.

The attention then turns to Madeleine herself, who doesn't appear to be the least bit nervous. Her introduction is confident. 'Hello, everyone. I'm so happy to be here after a chance encounter meeting Sylvie at the last WI meeting. I had no idea a local writing group existed, but I'm pleased I've found you as I think I may be able to be of help to some of you, as I'm sure you will be to me.'

'Whatever do you mean, pray tell?' prompts Joy, voicing all our thoughts.

We all lean forward with curiosity, waiting to hear what Madeleine has to say.

'I'm a cover designer,' she states. 'I mostly create non-fiction covers for self-help and business books and the like, but I've just started branching out into designing covers for novels – romance to start with a view to expanding into many different genres. So, if that's something anyone would be interested in, please get in touch. I'll give out my contact details at the end.'

As people murmur their interest, nodding and scribbling in notebooks, Sylvie clears her throat to take command of the floor once more. I wonder how she's going to react to Madeleine stealing her limelight, and whether she knew Madeleine's angle, if that's what she suspects it is, before inviting her along to our meeting.

'Thank you, Madeleine, how very interesting,' says Sylvie, setting her mug of coffee back down without having taken a sip. She clasps her hands together and regards our new member for a moment. 'I wasn't aware of your exact profession when we talked at the WI but I'm sure a few people here will be very eager to hear more. However, this is a writing group and not a place to pitch for business, so I do politely ask for any future dealings to be conducted between members privately. This is a space to share our creativity.' She smiles insincerely, thin eyebrows raised and beady eyes fixed on our newest member.

I could have predicted Sylvie's speech. She doesn't respond well to people being more successful than her in the writing and publishing arena and now that Madeleine can potentially help any of us become more polished authors with her professional cover design services, Sylvie seems a bit put out, despite the newly revealed existence of her second book.

Madeleine, strangely, doesn't look admonished in the slightest as she holds her hands up in an apology gesture to Sylvie, and I admire her assured attitude. If she stays in the group – if she is indeed *allowed* to stay in the group – I'm sure she'll add an extra tense dimension to it, which could be interesting.

'Are you currently writing at all, Madeleine?' I ask, in an attempt to ease the slightly stilted atmosphere which has now settled upon us.

'Not currently, no. I have written, in the past – short stories mostly, like Kenny – and really enjoyed it, but I seem to have lost my muse lately, which is also what I hope you'll all be able to help me with.'

'Been there,' states Lloyd, nodding emphatically.

'Well, I for one may well chat to you privately at a later time, darling!' confirms Joy, sneaking a sideways glance at Sylvie. I'm unable to stop myself from smiling.

Sylvie's face sets and darkens, and I know that it's going to be a short meeting today. I try to change the subject. 'I wonder where the other new member has got to. Did you get a message, Sylvie?'

'I don't know, Paige. My phone isn't surgically attached to my hand like so many,' she replies, fishing it out of her bag. She opens the flip case and squints at the screen. 'Oh, yes,' she announces. 'He's been good enough to send his apologies. He'll try to make it next week instead.'

'He? Ooh lovely, redress the gender balance a bit! Who is this gentleman, Sylvie? Spill the beans!' says Joy, forever the nosy parker.

'Well, from the brief telephone conversation I had with him, he sounds like a lovely young man who got our details from a flyer advertising the book fair.' She snaps her phone shut and drops it back in her bag, squinting as she tries to remember more of the "beans" that Joy has demanded. 'James something-beginning-with-L, I think. I didn't quite catch it.'

As Joy coos and comments, a strange tingling sensation starts in my stomach... surely it's not James Locksley?

Chapter Twelve

Aydan's due here in fifteen minutes and I'm frantically tidying the house, getting changed, weaving around Hardy, lighting candles and trying to keep an eye on the lasagne that's bubbling away in my ancient oven. Despite texting on Tuesday to say he'd have to stay on in Scotland, he surprised me today by announcing he doesn't have to work this weekend after all and suggested a quiet, belated Valentine's night in. He wants to Netflix and chill – literally – so I'm accommodating his request like a good girlfriend and providing comfort and sustenance while I'm at it. His house, which I've never seen and only recently discovered is near the marina, is apparently barely habitable – a "permanent before picture", so he says. It must be difficult to even begin making it homely when he's hardly ever there.

It feels weird us already being at the cosy night in stage after technically only one date, but I do like it. Him being here in the flesh will stop me thinking or worrying about other things so much, namely anonymous messages and another bookish man who's on my mind more than he should be, especially now that he could be a fellow writing group member.

Aydan arrives nearly half an hour later than planned. He looks a bit dishevelled, which is unusual from what I've seen of him so far. He's usually the epitome of a metrosexual man – clean finger-nailed and deliciously fragranced, despite frequenting dirty, dusty building sites. Today he's wearing what looks like an old jumper, combat trousers and glasses, and the ends of his mullet are curling around his collar. Not quite the squeaky clean, carefully coiffed and styled Aydan I'm used to in the flesh, but I don't dislike it.

'I didn't know you wore glasses,' I say, holding the door open as he kisses my cheek and hands me a bottle of wine. 'You look so different.'

'Modern-day Clark Kent,' he says, reaching down to fuss an excitable Hardy before following me through my modestly sized lounge diner to my galley kitchen at the back of the house. I place the bottle of wine on my melamine worktop while I check that the food is cooked and turn off the oven. He looks around the room. 'Nice place. It reminds me of the house I lived in with my mum when I was young. Pretty much the same size and layout.'

Probably the same era too, I think, given the extensive updating my little terrace needs. I note that it's the first time Aydan's mentioned family – we haven't had those kinds of talks yet and I'm not ready to volunteer any of my own family history either.

'Wine now?' I ask, reaching for the bottle, before casually redirecting the conversation to his lateness, which I'm interested in knowing the reason behind.

He apologises, explaining that he got caught up with a problem at his renovation project, then he takes the bottle from my hand, puts it down again and pulls me to him, folding me in his arms. He rests his chin on top of my head, pressing his warm body against me. I breathe him in and feel pleased he's here, but I get the impression something's not right.

'Thank you again for the beautiful Valentine's flowers you sent,' I say, hoping to override the tension I can sense. The last thing I want is any awkwardness. 'I can't remember the last time I got some, so they were a lovely surprise.' I glance at the vase of yellow roses on the dining table, above where Hardy is currently sprawled, and recall my shock when they arrived. Not only at the romantic gesture but also because I wondered how Aydan got my address. After a moment of stomach-plunging panic that I could be found so easily, I remembered it was on the proofreading invoice I sent him when I began work on his book. That probably made it easier for him to get my phone number too. Considering I'm meant to be keeping myself safe, I've become a bit lackadaisical lately. Yet all Aydan's done is gone out of his way to show me he cares and to prove his interest in me. I'm amazed and touched he's this keen so soon.

He holds me a little bit tighter but doesn't reply and a few moments pass in silence. Enough time for my thoughts to flip from appreciating his gestures to worrying that perhaps he intends to break up with me. Maybe he doesn't want to try as hard as he has been, after all. Maybe I'm not actually worth the extra effort.

'I can't stay tonight, after all, Paige,' he says eventually.

'Oh?' I enquire, pulling back and looking up at him. I steel myself for the impending death knell.

'Yeah, I need to get back to site first thing tomorrow. I got a phone call on the way home – even more problems have cropped up as a consequence of the original problem.' He releases me, takes off his glasses and runs a hand down his face, holding his bearded chin and looking at me apologetically with kind, tired eyes.

'I'm knackered, Paige, but I need to be there to muck in. It's not fair to leave the others to do it all, they're doing me a favour agreeing to overtime as it is. I hate to eat and run but I'm going to have to. It was either that or not seeing you at all, and I didn't want to not see you.'

'So you're not breaking up with me?' I ask.

'What? No, of course not, AC!' he says, laughing. He gives me a big squeeze. I feel instantly relieved and reassured.

'It's okay, honestly,' I reassure him in return. 'I admire how dedicated you are to your work.'

He smiles down at me then kisses me softly on the nose. Now he's here I realise how much I've missed him and a fresh wave of guilt washes over me as I recall my zealous interest in James Locksley, but I still can't stop myself from asking Aydan about him.

'Oh, by the way, I saw your friend James the other day when I was walking Hardy. He said to say hello,' I lie as I open the oven and extract the potato wedges.

Aydan tries to reach over to pinch one and I nudge him out of the way with my hip.

'Good things come to those who wait,' I admonish.

He raises his eyebrows and smirks cheekily, and I can't help but grin back, glad the mood has lightened.

'Mmm, it all smells so good. I'm starving,' he says. The lasagne is looking decidedly well done but he seems grateful I made the effort. 'Who said to say hello?' he asks.

'James Locksley. The guy you spoke to when we were at the restaurant on our first date. He says you met at a property auction in Leeds,' I state, only remembering that nugget of information as I voice it. It's been over three years since I left the city but I still shiver at the mere mention of the place, which is now forever tainted. I wonder at Aydan's connection with Leeds for the first time. 'Did you already have property there too? Or were you just interested in buying in that area?' I ask, trying to sound casual.

'I'm interested in you.' He snakes his arms round my waist as I finish transferring the rest of the charred food from the oven to the worktop.

'Smooth,' I say as he nuzzles my neck, wondering why he's evading my questions. He probably thinks I'm prying. I may be his girlfriend in name, but I obviously have yet to earn full disclosure status. Fair enough: at least that means he won't be expecting chapter and verse on my past either. He certainly won't be getting it.

I feel him nip my skin with his teeth and I flinch before quickly detaching myself to fill our plates with my decidedly burnt offerings, trying my best to disguise my distaste. I'm not into biting, however playful he thinks he's being. I don't want to ruin the mood by addressing it, but I don't want him to do it again later either. I already know he's quite vigorous in bed, or at least he was that first time. I need to vocalise–

'Paige?'

Hearing my name pulls me out of my overthinking spiral. Aydan's looking at me expectantly and I realise I've missed what he said while I've been busy in my own head.

'I asked how the book's coming along?' he says, and I immediately soften. He might have sidestepped my enquiries about his work but I'm grateful for his unwavering interest in mine. And what does a gentle bite matter anyway? It's not as if he's a vampire! I put a smile back on my face.

'Well, I'm still heavily into the revision process and I've got some work to do for a new client, so you'd be in my way tomorrow anyway,' I tease.

'Good job I'm going soon then, isn't it?' He winks before leaning back against the worktop. 'Anyway, tell me more about this new client. Shall I finally pour the wine?' He nods at the bottle.

'Thank you,' I say, again amazed that there's not only a gorgeous man in my kitchen, but one who wants to pour me wine and listen to me talk. Quite the contrast to the past few years. 'Well, this new client may lead to a contact in the publishing industry too,' I begin. 'They've offered to pass my manuscript on to an editor they know,' I explain as I finish serving the food.

Aydan unscrews the wine cap and gets two glasses out of the cupboard I point to. 'That sounds great, Paige, but I thought you wanted to revise your book a few times before letting anyone else see it?'

'I do. Well, I did, but it's really starting to stress me out so I'm wondering whether it's worth submitting it after one pass so I can get the publishing ball rolling sooner rather than later. What do you think?'

'I'm hardly the right person to ask, given that my own editor sent me right off-kilter.' He grins, referring to our previous – and extremely brief – working relationship before we began dating, the attraction impossible to ignore. 'No, seriously, you should go for it.'

I stop what I'm doing and study him, this exhausted man working long hours and now weekends, who once dreamt of becoming a published author himself. 'Do you regret it, pressing pause on your book for me?' I ask seriously as he sips his drink.

He swallows and shakes his head, smiling. 'No way. The book can wait but I couldn't wait for you. I still wish you'd let me pay you something for the work you did do though.'

'You can pay me in kind,' I reply as I lean over to kiss my sweet-talking boyfriend, deciding to make a concerted effort to focus my thoughts on food and wine and Netflix and chilling, and away from James Locksley, for now.

The Doubt Creeps In

It was a staff meeting, apparently. A staff meeting at eight o'clock in the evening. After hours. She knew it was a lie and she knew he was a liar, then. Was it his first lie? Her brain obligingly recalled other little details from past weeks, foraged for more examples, yanked them out and held them up against the light, examining them for signs of trouble. She saw them too, now.

'Who's texting you?' she asked from the other end of the settee as his phone buzzed with texts which he smiled at before replying to. They no longer lay entwined like sloths.

'Hmm?' he responded, not really paying any attention to her.

'Who keeps texting you, Mr Popular?' she repeated, helping herself to another biscuit, trying to keep her voice light, playful.

'Oh, just work stuff. Banter.' He kept his focus on his phone, thumb moving deftly across the miniature keypad.

She hadn't realised he knew any of his colleagues well enough yet to exchange "banter" with them by text. He had started a new job as a car salesman at the local Vauxhall garage the week before, his first job since they had met. She hadn't worked out his motives for getting it yet; she suspected pressure from his mother, or maybe his stepfather, finally trying to force financial independence on him. Bit late, really.

'I'll be late home again tomorrow, by the way,' he said.

'Right. Why?' she asked.

'Customer's collecting their new car after they've finished work.'

He turned towards her, appraising her slowly, eyes traveling up and down her plumper-than-it-used-to-be body, before deliberately settling his gaze on the biscuit in her hand.

'Are you eating all of those, Miss Piggy? I'd lay off them a bit if I were you.'

He left the room then, snatching up the remaining biscuits and taking his phone with him, retreating to his dark office his password-protected computers, for the rest of the night.

— *Descent into Deceit*

Chapter Thirteen

I t's Wednesday again and everyone has arrived promptly at Lloyd's handsome detached house in Newland Park, near Hull University. I wasn't sure Madeleine would want to – or even be allowed to – return after Sylvie's telling off last week, but she's here too, matching Joy in the cheerful stakes and greeting everyone pleasantly.

Sylvie's positioned herself at the head of Lloyd's dining table, as expected, and the rest of us have taken our places around her, saying our hellos and retrieving notebooks and pens and diaries from our bags whilst Lloyd goes off to rustle up the coffee in Sylvie's travelling cafetière. I wonder briefly if she brings it to be controlling and selfish or genuinely helpful and generous.

I'm anxious today – Lloyd is no doubt going to ask me about the progress I've made on his book after we agreed I'd make a start on it this week. I don't know how to tell him I think it needs a lot more work than just a proofread, which should only happen once the book is in the best shape it can be, after everything that needs to be revised has been revised. I would never insensitively criticise any author and as this is his first attempt at fiction, at writing anything in years, I must tread carefully. I'm also worried about the repercussions of being honest. He may retract his offer of passing my manuscript to his editor contact and although I haven't asked him to do that yet, I'm becoming increasingly excited about the prospect of getting some objective professional feedback. But I'm also still terrified of getting some objective professional feedback, given the storyline was my real life.

Lloyd returns bearing the huge vessel of coffee and places it on the table next to the cups which are already laid out. Looking around while Joy kindly plays waitress for myself and my fellow members I notice how tidy and clean his dining room is and how it still bears his ex-wife's touch. Although I gathered they divorced a few years ago, it looks as though she still inhabits the space due to the feminine décor and furnishings and ornaments. There's still a framed picture of their wedding day on the sideboard too; it seems Lloyd has a hard time moving on from more than his writing and I feel even more nervous about giving him my thoughts on his novel.

Madeleine thanks Joy for filling her cup and Joy points a red talon at Madeleine's notebook which has one of those photo covers. From my side of the table it looks like a picture of a beaming toddler wearing dungarees. 'Ooh, who's this cheeky little chap – a grandson perhaps?' asks Joy.

'No, it's my son when he was younger. He's a strapping thirty-three-year-old now.' Madeleine smiles at the photo affectionately.

'Absolutely gorgeous!' states Joy. 'And what a coincidence – my son's thirty-three now too.'

'My Alexander's supposedly twenty-nine but you'd think he was still in his teens the way he carries on,' Renee interjects, rolling her eyes.

'Do you have any pictures of your sons?' Madeleine asks Joy and Renee kindly.

The other two mothers nod, and Joy darts back to her seat as Renee forages in her bag, clearly only too happy to proudly share photos of their own offspring. I'm interested too, particularly in what Joy's son looks like, having seen myriad framed family images at Renee's house already.

However, before either woman can produce their pictures, Sylvie calls the meeting to action, commenting that personal matters can wait until after business matters. Joy pulls a comedic naughty face and hooks her handbag back over her chair. Now that I know both Madeleine and Joy have sons only slightly older than me, I hope they won't be attempting to matchmake, the way Renee did with Alexander. I've been having enough trouble trying to focus on one man as it is.

Sylvie begins by recapping all the book fair details for the umpteenth time. It's drawing ever closer and she is eager to ensure arrangements are airtight, despite having sent another six emails about it since it was discussed at Kenny's house last Wednesday. I've finished the workshop plan outline and we're all au fait with the running order for the day, but we all indulge her nonetheless, at least on the face of it.

I let my mind wander during Sylvie's monologue. Talk of the book fair, which is happening in just a couple of weeks, reminds me about James again and I conjure up his image: strong, smiling, dog-loving, book-writing, sexy-as-hell James Locksley. I can't help but imagine him as the protagonist in the romance books I've taken to reading, which is making them even more enjoyable yet distracting at the same time. The brief time Aydan and I spent together last Friday helped to push all thoughts of James to the far recesses of my mind and, for the few hours we had, I was completely absorbed in my boyfriend and our lovely, relaxing evening (without any more amorous red flags triggering me, thankfully). But James seems to have jostled to the forefront again since then.

I shake my head and rejoin the conversation, reminding myself that James Locksley is nothing more than a schoolgirl crush. He hasn't turned up today either so Sylvie's "James something-beginning-with-L" might not have been him, after all. It's my relationship with Aydan that's real, albeit time restricted due to him working away, and I need to stop fantasising about another man.

As the meeting finally draws to a close and people are shrugging their coats back on and draining the last of their coffees, I look up to see Lloyd signalling to me to wait a moment and I resign myself to having the conversation I've been dreading. I've never been comfortable delivering news people might not want to hear as the introvert in me always shies away from any possible confrontation.

As Sylvie passes me to pop to the loo, I linger over the task of putting my notebook and pen away as the others file out amid a chorus of goodbyes and Joy's usual refrain: 'Toodle pip!' I walk through to the hallway, coat on, bag across my body, sending a clear visual signal that I can't stay long, as Lloyd pushes the door shut behind our fellow group members, effectively trapping me inside.

'I won't pester you for progress on my book just yet, Paige,' he begins, completely surprising me. 'I just wanted to ask what you've decided – if you have yet – about me passing your manuscript to my editor contact? I've already put the feelers out. She's got some unexpected space in her schedule and is happy to take a look at it for you in the next few weeks.'

I'm stunned for a minute, not only at Lloyd's patience with regards his own manuscript, but at the possibility of feedback on my own novel within mere weeks – usually editors are booked up months in advance, especially those still working at the coalface of a publishing house itself. For a split second I think about what a shame it is that Lloyd's too reticent to present his own book to his contact, then quickly remember my own thoughts about it and how delicate his damaged reputation is. Perhaps it's for the best he leaves it with me and doesn't risk anyone else seeing it, I think savagely. As for my own novel, however, I suddenly realise I've got absolutely nothing to lose by passing it on. I'm not washed up, I don't have the pressure of expectation on me and I'm not too jaded to try, so why not give it a go? My only worry is, what might Lloyd expect in return? In my experience, genuine favours are extremely rare, if not completely extinct.

'Paige?' He jolts me out of my swirling thoughts. 'What do you think?'

'I... I think I would like you to pass it on, Lloyd,' I manage to say as the wonder of possibility engulfs me, overpowering my cynicism. 'I'll speed up my revisions on the hard copy, make the changes on my digital copy and send it to you very soon.'

'No problem,' he replies. 'Happy to help.'

I smile at him as he opens the door, and I practically skip over the front step and onto the path. As I turn back to thank him, I see a curious face peeping through the gap in the downstairs toilet doorway. Nosy old Sylvie, yet again. Did she hear our conversation?

Chapter Fourteen

Hardy and I are up and out early on Thursday morning. He bounds after the ball I've just thrown for him in a drizzly, deserted Westfield Park and I feel my phone vibrate in my pocket. It's a text from Aydan, informing me he's working all weekend — definitely this time. His apology is profuse with a heartfelt promise to make it up to me, depicted by cheeky emojis. I sigh, feeling strangely disappointed and out of sorts. I was looking forward to a distraction this weekend as much as the enjoyment of spending time with my boyfriend since we reconnected last Friday during our romantic night in.

I tap out an emoji reply to Aydan — three unhappy faces — as Hardy begins to yap excitedly. Another dog is on the field and Hardy's off-lead. He's sometimes so unpredictable meeting new dogs that my heart rate rises as I scan the area, but I soon spot him playing happily with a red setter. Red. Which only means one thing — James Locksley is here too.

He's walking towards me beneath the damp canopy of trees, one hand clenching Red's lead, the other raised in greeting. It's a very pleasing sight indeed and my heart rate rises again, but for a very different reason. The familiar jittery feeling extends from my stomach until my whole body is shivering despite the warmth. An echo of a familiar voice tells me I must look a state in my wellies and big coat. I ignore it; it holds no power over me anymore.

'We really must stop meeting like this.' He smiles as he approaches and again goes in for a kiss on my cheek even though I've got my hood up. 'How are you?' he asks as he stands back, at ease, which is completely at odds with how I now feel. I make the effort to pull myself together – why does he always have this effect on me?

'Good, great, I'm okay. Hi, it's good to see you again,' I babble. 'And Red, of course. How are you?'

'All the better for seeing you and Hardy on this miserable morning,' he replies, arm extending wide to signal how wet the February weather is, and how quiet the park is. We're the only dog walkers here. The only other person in the vicinity is a dedicated jogger doing laps around the perimeter path. 'This is my only chance to be social before I'm confined to my lonely home office.'

Our eyes meet and he holds my gaze for a few seconds longer than necessary. Or am I imagining it through the soft drizzle?

'I know what you mean about feeling confined,' I say, blushing, glancing again at Hardy and Red gambolling together. 'I've been cooped up at home, revising my book and getting it ready to send off to an editor at a publishing house. It's nearly ready to submit.'

'Paige, that's brilliant,' he says, clearly genuinely pleased for me. 'I remember when I held the same dream – the excitement, the anticipation, the potential career change. Who wouldn't want to write books for a living? Best job in the world, if you ask me.'

I'm taken aback by his enthusiasm. I wanted common ground and I've certainly found it.

'Hey we should celebrate you nearly finishing your novel. How about a drink, somewhere that isn't Westfield Park? We can chat about books to our hearts' content, author to author.'

'Now?' I squeak, caught completely off guard.

He laughs again, a pleasing sound. 'No, work beckons, I'm afraid, and I meant a proper drink. How about tomorrow tonight, if you're up for it? 7pm at that new little cocktail place just off Willerby Square?'

I know exactly where he means; there was an article about it online. It looks very cosy with its low lights and dark décor. The exhilaration stuns me so intensely I can only blink rapidly in amazement, astounded by his offer. I assumed he meant a quick coffee from the greasy spoon across the road. Yet a part of me should be appalled. We've barely spoken ten sentences to each other since we met at the restaurant my boyfriend took me to just a couple of weeks ago. Plus, as he seems so slick at this, I very much doubt he's a beginner at asking random women out in parks. Yet he's not looking at me with anything other than hopeful expectation, and as he knows I've got a boyfriend, this can't be anything other than a friendly invitation, can it?

I gather my composure as I regard him, conflicting emotions battling within me. I can't pretend I haven't fantasised about a scenario like this, and more, whatever his intentions might be.

'Okay,' I hear myself say eventually.

'See you there then.' He smiles, nods once, whistles for Red and then walks away, arrangement in place. What have I just agreed to? An innocent bookish chat between new author friends, or something more?

Chapter Fifteen

I've spent longer getting ready to meet James than for any of my dates with Aydan. Despite trying to convince myself otherwise, I know exactly what tonight means to me and I've not just readily agreed, I've wholeheartedly embraced it with a longer than usual walk for Hardy before a thorough shaving, plucking and moisturising routine in the bathroom. I've even messaged Aydan and lied about having a migraine and needing an early night to prevent him from calling or texting while I'm out. I'm a terrible, selfish person who is prepared to do terrible, selfish things.

As I enter the bar in what constitutes for glad rags in my limited wardrobe, I feel a sudden flush of foolishness – I'm meeting a stranger to all intents and purposes, whose phone number I don't even have. This could be a joke and if it's not a joke but isn't what I expect it to be, no one even knows I'm here. This isn't the first time I've done this, and that previous encounter ended up changing the trajectory of my life. I didn't tell anyone who I was meeting that night either. Not Julia and certainly not my grandad. I had to sneak out of the house and although I thought the risk was worth it, the beating I would have endured if I had been caught might have saved me a lot of time, trouble and heartache of a much worse kind.

Anyway, who would I tell if anything goes awry tonight – Aydan? I'm sure he'd be delighted to hear I've met one of his acquaintances behind his back after lying to him about not feeling great and immediately volunteer to drive back from Scotland to save me, if necessary.

My sarcastic thoughts stop as I see James at a table near the back of the narrow bar, one hand on the stem of his beer bottle. He must have only recently arrived. The exposed brick walls, low ceiling and lantern lighting give the place an industrial, underground atmosphere, which seems fitting for our furtive rendezvous. As I approach him, he stands to greet me and plants a soft kiss on my cheek. I feel slightly light-headed already.

'You look amazing,' he says, appraising me appreciatively as I remove my coat, letting the compliment float in the charged air for a moment. It's obvious how much effort I've made, compared to the windswept, casual version of me he saw in the park yesterday.

I thank him, feeling rebellious and giddy to be taking back some control of my life, finally. It's about time I began to live a little, first being brave enough to set my manuscript free and now meeting a new "friend" in a bar. What the repercussions of these actions may be, I've yet to find out, but I think I'm overdue some luck, for a change. I think the risks may well be worth it.

James looks as good as ever, the soft light catching the distinguished crinkles around those hypnotic eyes. I take the seat facing towards the front of the restaurant, as always. Although I don't choose to make a habit of evenings out in public places, this little bar feels tucked away enough to not have to keep a close watch on the door for a change, just in case.

'Drink?' he enquires.

I throw caution to the wind and ask for a mojito, which he

orders for me at the bar. As I wait, I glance over at him. He's got one foot on a bar-stool's footrest and is tapping his fingers gently on the bar as if playing a tune. His arse looks great in his jeans.

He returns with my drink as well as another beer for himself. I notice it's non-alcoholic. The ice-cold tang of my mojito makes me shiver after I take a sip, and it's a pleasing sensation. I glance at James as I place my glass on the table. Considering how chatty he's been in the park, I sense he's slightly more reserved tonight. Maybe he's regretting asking me out now I'm here. The thought makes me immediately self-conscious, which in turn, makes me nervous. I need to initiate conversation if he's not going to.

'Bit of a weird question,' I begin, sounding more upbeat than I now feel, 'but you haven't joined a writing group recently, have you?'

He takes a swig of his beer, nodding then smiling as he sets it down. 'As a matter of fact, I have,' he confirms. 'What can I say? You inspired me to give writing another go.'

He looks at me, obviously registering the expression on my face – I've never been able to hide my feelings well and he must see I'm a bit taken aback. Is it genuinely a coincidence that the writing group he's suddenly decided to join is mine, especially after I mentioned us having a stall at the book fair? I feel a prickle of something I can't quite define.

'Oh God, is it yours?' he asks, suddenly, genuinely concerned. 'If it is, just tell me and I won't intrude. It's just, after our first chat, I realised how much I miss it. I'd love to write another book and I've got loads of ideas but work and... stuff... keeps getting in the way and I haven't made time for it.' He stops, looks at me and half laughs, rubbing the back of his neck. 'Look, I don't want to make you feel awkward in any way. I've already missed a couple of meetings I said I would go to, so just say the word if you think it's too weird. I'm not a stalker though, honestly.' He lifts both hands up, palms towards me as if to prove his integrity.

I study him for a few moments, past experience rendering me incapable of knowing if or when someone is being truthful, my gut feeling a permanent traitor. I consider my response: regardless of his motives, it's just a writing group – what harm can it do? On the other hand, we're sitting in a bar, together, and my motives for being here aren't exactly pure, so would seeing each other every week be wise? The thing is, I'm not entirely sure I can be wise where James is concerned.

'No, join the group, you'll be very welcome,' I say. 'But watch out for Sylvie – and Joy. They're both forces to be reckoned with and desperate for a new male member!' I widen my eyes in horror as I realise the inappropriateness of what I've just said. 'Oh God, I'm... I didn't mean.' I press my lips together, mortified, but he just chuckles. 'I'm sure Kenny and Lloyd will be grateful to be slightly less outnumbered too.'

He mimes wiping his brow and breathing a sigh of relief. 'I was worried there for a moment,' he admits. 'Thank you for the approval. I'm really looking forward to being around other writers on a regular basis.' He looks at me pointedly and I feel my face heat. 'Cheers to my initiation hopefully next Wednesday then.' He picks up his bottle again and touches it to my glass as the prickle subsides into something pleasingly positive.

Over the next hour or so, the bar remains fairly quiet, but our conversation picks up pace. We warm up to each other by chatting about our jobs, our dogs and ourselves, and each newly revealed fact strengthens my attraction to James. However, he hasn't mentioned Aydan at all yet, and I certainly haven't brought up the fact that he's out with another man's girlfriend.

It happens much sooner than I expect it to. His hand moves to rest on my knee, and then after a minute or two, his thumb begins slowly circling my naked outer thigh. Neither of us openly acknowledges this fluid, rhythmic touch yet I am deliciously hyper aware of it. A memory of another hand on my leg surprises me with its vividness, but it is not a kind recollection. It is of a clench, a squeeze, an inflicted force that took my breath away with its intention to harm.

I flinch slightly, which James perhaps mistakes as a shudder of disgust and deftly moves his hand back to his almost empty third bottle of beer. I immediately and gently reposition it back where it was and he smiles at me, his chipped front tooth making an appearance, his eyes showing his appreciation of my permission to continue touching my body.

Strangely, Aydan infiltrates my thoughts, but not in the way he should. I'm thinking of him but not about him, fully aware, despite my cocktail-influenced state that I don't care about being unfaithful to him tonight. I used to care how I behaved – I was made to care about how I behaved; a "good" fiancée, a "good" granddaughter – but not anymore. Now, I realise I am free to choose, and tonight I already choose James.

A ringing interrupts my conviction and as I look down at my bag, despite knowing my phone is on silent, I'm aware of James bringing his own phone out of his pocket. He glances at me after checking the name displayed. I see it too: *Sofia*.

'I'm so sorry,' he whispers. 'I'll be back in a minute.'

I watch him walk towards the doorway and just catch a curt 'What is it?' as the phone reaches his ear. Instantly my writer's imagination conjures up her character: a beautiful Italian woman, sophisticated and mature, with no interest in playing games and no knowledge of being involved in one as her cad of a boyfriend (husband?) entertains a bookish younger model, albeit no match for her. Or perhaps she does sense something is off, so she's ringing in an attempt to garner attention, battle plans drawn up and wronged wife weapons sharpened, ready to execute him if she has to. Or me, for that matter.

Yet who am I to talk? What am I doing? Cheating isn't me and justifying it because of my past is nothing short of shameful. I suddenly feel utterly ridiculous, an actress in a role I shouldn't have taken. I begin to gather my bag and coat as James reappears.

'Paige?' He's frowning, whether because of the phone call or seeing me making a move to leave so suddenly, I don't know.

'I need to go; this was a mistake.' The classic illicit date missive falls from my lips as I wrap myself in my coat and attempt to fasten the buttons. My hand-eye coordination is affected due to the many mojitos I've consumed, and my trembling fingers can't seem to complete the simple task. He notices and wraps one of his hands over mine, waiting patiently for me to look at him. I eventually do.

'Paige, what's wrong?' he asks. I search his eyes for any telltale signs of bastardry and I'm strangely disappointed to find none, only genuine concern, which makes no sense in my intoxicated state. I want to be furious with him, as furious as I currently am with myself, for engaging in this silly little dance of mutual attraction, yet I'm not. Unable to make sense of my conflicting thoughts and emotions, let alone verbalise them, I can only shake my head and look away.

'Come on,' he says, reading the change in atmosphere and perhaps understanding the reason behind it. 'I'll call a taxi.'

As we wait, shivering in the doorway of the bar we have just spent an intimate couple of hours inside, something silent shifts between us and he leans in to kiss me as naturally as if he's done it a hundred times before. And I let him. He's gentle and warm, yet I can sense his strength from his embrace. Our lips meet again and again, at first unfamiliar and tentative, but as we find an exquisite rhythm, I consciously let go of all thoughts of Aydan, and Sofia, and all I can think of, and feel, is James.

Chapter Sixteen

March 2017

It's been five long days since I saw James. Since I tasted James. I haven't felt an intensity like that before, especially not just from a kiss, and it was exhilarating. I felt charged, like my whole body was buzzing from within. But the guilt has been seeping back in like a noxious gas ever since, weaving itself around my brain, permeating my thoughts with vicious remarks and recriminations.

I'm struggling with it. I shouldn't have had those cocktails. Alcohol always makes me carefree and loosens my guard. I need to be more cautious and considerate. Aydan doesn't deserve my infidelity. He messaged that night when I returned home, the text so perfectly timed as I exited the back seat of the taxi – alone, I must add – that for one crazy moment I pictured him blanketed by the shadows, watching me. Spying on his liar of a girlfriend.

> Hey AC, missing you more than you know.
> Hope you're feeling better and getting plenty of
> beauty sleep, not that you need it! Looking
> forward to an update on the book (and more!)
> on Friday. A xxx

I know better than anyone about the mental torture when you suspect an affair, so I've decided I'm going to nip things in the bud with James today, after the writing group. I've purposely not walked Hardy around Westfield Park so that I wouldn't run into him, but I can't flake out of the meeting today, not this close to the book fair. My stomach swirls at the thought of seeing him again but I daren't incur Sylvie's wrath.

I arrive at Renee's three-storey end terrace in Marlborough Avenue, one of the four tree-lined avenues not far from Westfield Park, near Hull's city centre. It's a lovely area, and Renee has a gorgeous house. Being early is a calculated move designed to make me feel calmer and more in control when James arrives.

Renee flings the door open looking decidedly harassed and ushers me into her sitting room before zipping off upstairs on an errand obviously pertaining to her son, Alexander, given the volume she hollers his name and the heavy stamp of her feet on the steps.

Having fully expected Sylvie to already be here, despite my own premature appearance, I'm surprised to find myself alone in the room. I settle myself in one of the two too-big-for-the-space, oxblood leather Chesterfield armchairs, adjacent to the Victorian fireplace, which is disappointingly camouflaged due to a cluttered mantel and hearth. From my seat I can see the paved front path through the big swags-and-tails-framed bay window. It's a prime spot to be able to see the other members arrive and to not have to sit closely to anyone else. Exactly as I had hoped.

My senses are on high alert, anticipating the rush of adrenaline upon seeing James again. As I take in Renee's cobwebbed high ceilings and dusty wooden floors, as well as the overflowing bookshelves and dark, heavy, mahogany furniture, I remind myself of the reason I am here – for *my* writing group –

and scold myself yet again for jeopardising my place in this little nook I've found, for nothing more than an infatuation.

I'll simply have to leave, find another group. But James was the last to join so shouldn't it be last in, first out? What if I have to admit to our flirtations and recent date, creating an awkward situation amongst the other members – would they choose me over him? Or would we both be cast out like unnecessary adjectives in an otherwise perfect sentence? I feel so tired, exhausted by my own constant overthinking.

My runaway train of thought thankfully glides back to a manageable pace as I spy Joy and Sylvie approaching the door. I hear the bell and wait for Renee to answer it. A few moments pass and the bell sounds again. It's clear Renee is still otherwise engaged so I leave my safe seat to let my fellow members in, hoping Renee won't mind.

'Darling, you're an early bird!' greets Joy as I swing open the door. Sylvie is clutching the now infamous cafetière like a middle-class door-to-door saleswoman.

'Renee's dealing with something upstairs,' I explain as I step back, making room for them to come in. The hallway is wide and would be spacious, but it's so densely cluttered and filled with so many pieces of furniture creating a slalom of sharp corners that it feels quite claustrophobic. The beautiful stained-glass porthole window to the left of the front door is partially obscured by a glass display cabinet housing a collection of what appears to be pewter dragon ornaments, each one bearing a different coloured jewel, and, quite at odds with its cabinet companions, a dusty set of Royal Family memorabilia.

Joy and Sylvie shuffle past me and onwards as I signal the way to the sitting room, shutting the door in their wake as Renee appears at the top of the stairs.

'Never have a son!' she warns in exasperation as she descends, fists clenched, face flushed.

'Joy and Sylvie are here,' I inform her by way of reply.

'Has she brought that bloody cafetière?' Renee asks in a stage whisper, not needing to specify who "she" is. I nod, smiling. Renee sighs and, as per expectation, proceeds to relieve Sylvie of her wares.

As I enter the sitting room again, I see that Joy is now sitting in the seat I vacated and Sylvie is in its twin, and I realise with a slight panic that I have no choice but to settle on the huge Chesterfield sofa buffering the wall opposite the fireplace, behind the door. I no longer have a view of the front footpath and if James arrives next there is every chance he will sit next to me, which is the last thing I want.

My heart rate increases again at the thought of being in such close proximity to him after Friday night and it is all I can do not to make my excuses and leave immediately; the fear of running into him outside greater only than the agonising wait for him to appear inside.

'Are you all right, Paige? You look a bit skittish,' observes Sylvie, astutely.

As if reprimanded by a teacher in a classroom, I make the effort to rein in my skittishness and sit up a little straighter.

'I'm fine,' I lie, my voice pitchy. 'I've just got a lot on today, what with my book and other work... I might have to leave early, actually.' I silently congratulate myself for the lifeline, mentally preparing to scarper as soon as I can. Back home to Hardy and the safety of my own four walls.

Sylvie doesn't respond to my comment but looks at her watch pointedly. 'Where are the boys? It's bang on ten o'clock. Our new member James isn't coming today but Kenny and Lloyd are usually punctual.' As if on cue, the doorbell rings again.

Sylvie's insistence on referring to Kenny and Lloyd as

"boys" completely bypasses my funny bone as my brain only picks up the information about James.

'James isn't coming?' I ask, far too loudly and with far too much interest.

Sylvie and Joy exchange the briefest of looks. 'No, he sends his apologies,' replies Sylvie.

'Did he say why he wasn't coming?' In for a penny, in for a pound, I think as the words leave my mouth like an unpreventable regurgitation of something unpleasant, knowing I'm in danger of embarrassing myself but physically unable to contain it

'No, Paige, he didn't. Why do you ask?' Sylvie's eyebrows pop up to her silver hairline as she looks at me questioningly.

I sag back into the Chesterfield sofa, merely shaking my head in response as the doorbell chimes, signalling the arrival of "the boys".

'Madeleine isn't coming today either, or any other week for that matter. She feels this group is not for her after all, and I must admit, I'm inclined to agree,' Sylvie announces with a haughty sniff, although her voice sounds very far away.

'Darling, is something the matter? You seem very disappointed about James not attending today. Do you know him?' Joy enquires, her expressive face full of curiosity and concern.

I would make a hopeless witness; my answer is no doubt plastered all over my face, audible in my tone and obvious in my body language. I need to try to salvage this, quickly. I sit forward again. 'No, no,' I lie with a forced cheeriness. 'I was just looking forward to welcoming another new member, even more so now Madeleine's dropped out. Excuse me, I'm just popping to the loo.'

I leave the room as briskly as possible, squashing myself up against the door jamb as Kenny and Lloyd navigate their way past me into the sitting room, whilst saying their hellos. Renee waits for them to file in so she can head back towards the kitchen. She sees me waiting.

'Paige, the downstairs loo is out of order, go upstairs – first floor, first door on the left. Alexander should finally be done in there now he's used all of the hot water – again.' She rolls her eyes.

I thank her and retrace the steps she took when she shot off upstairs earlier. I look upwards at the immense height of the three-storey house, feeling envious yet slightly sorrowful as the place has clearly been neglected. Instead of the beauty, all I see are scuffs and scratches and clutter and cobwebs adorning its ageing skin and bones.

As I reach the first-floor landing, the bathroom door is practically wrenched from its frame and I'm suddenly standing face to face with an astonishingly good-looking, fresh-smelling, wet-haired man-boy wearing nothing but a towel. Time suspends as I simply stare at him – obviously Renee's son, Alexander. He has the most incredible green eyes I have ever seen.

'What the fuck are you looking at?' he snarls before pushing past me and disappearing through one of the other doors, slamming it shut in his wake. Stunned, I try to process what has just happened, struggling to equate lovely, unassuming Renee with such a rude offspring who is clearly more attractive on the outside than on the inside.

The clatter of a coffee tray from the hallway below reminds me of my mission upstairs and two minutes later I return to the sitting room. Renee is pouring the drinks and as I take my seat next to Kenny on the sofa, I am passed a cup of hot coffee, which I accept, determined not to mention the surly young man above our heads, or James, for the duration of the meeting, despite my distracted brain now being full of them both.

Consequences

She would come home to the cold house they shared after her menial, mindless job, and the detritus of the day would be littered around him – microwaveable cartons, biscuit crumbs and used, sticky tissues – in his permanently closed-curtained bedroom-turned-office, the air stale and heavy with coffee breath and absorbed secrets. As well as his absent mother's money, the profit from her own house sale was subsidising his unemployed existence. She paid a chunk of the mortgage, but he paid no attention to her whatsoever anymore.

He would always minimise whatever was on his screen or close the door against her questions and prying eyes and she would retreat, wary of the physical consequences of his temper should she dare to speak out of turn.

'How's your day been?' Careful not to externalise her weary sigh or scathing observations, she chanced the loaded question.

He didn't even acknowledge her, attention fixed on his phone, the screen light illuminating his face menacingly in the little box room. He looked like a teenager, gadget crazy and sulky, annoyed at a parental presence spoiling his fun.

'I'm going out in ten,' he informed her, curtly, after a few moments, not even lifting his gaze.

Relief and disappointment sat on top of each other in her stomach, like oil and water, making it churn.

'Right,' she said. Then, 'Where?'

He finally looked at her.

'Somewhere more fucking interesting than here with someone more fucking interesting than you.'

— *Descent into Deceit*

Chapter Seventeen

It's Friday and Aydan's coming home tonight, or rather, he's supposed to be coming to mine, but I'm going to surprise him at his place a bit earlier in an effort to steer my love life back on track. I've had a couple of days to process my emotions following James not turning up to the writing group on Wednesday after our kiss last week, and I've decided the best course of action is just to do nothing where he is concerned and concentrate on mine and Aydan's relationship. James clearly thinks the same as he hasn't been in touch with me either.

I inwardly cringe as I again remember the surge of challenging emotions I experienced, and dealt badly with, at Renee's: crushing disappointment when Sylvie stated that James would be absent again, followed swiftly by excruciating embarrassment that I had obviously misread things between us, and then utter bewilderment immediately after the sudden, strange encounter with Renee's son Alexander on the landing. Since then, I've vowed to treat Aydan – the one man who isn't acting suspiciously lately – with a bit more respect. My guilt over James is still nibbling ferociously at me like a piranha, and I must do what I can to override it.

I already know that Aydan's house is close to the marina – a small two-up two-down townhouse on Victoria Dock with an amazing view across the River Humber even post-sunset like today, apparently. I wouldn't know as I've never been inside. The morning after our first night together following our restaurant date, a night punctuated with fizzing flutes of sweet champagne and then tantalising touches, I drove him home to get changed before he had to leave for Scotland. After exiting the car, he gave me a wink and raised his hand in a wave as I drove away. I smile at the memory as I pull up and park in one of the designated bays opposite the row of four townhouses. I think one of the middle two is his. I'm pretty sure it was second from the left.

Illuminated by a lone street lamp, the outside of the house shows all the signs of a busy, barely-there occupant – a weed-filled path, faded and splintering woodwork, and broken vertical blinds behind grubby windows. The hip-height brick wall separating the front garden from its right-hand neighbour's looks like it's barely survived a kicking as it tapers off halfway to just a collection of broken bricks sprawled beside the narrow path to the front door. One of the tarnished brass numbers on the door itself has come loose and is hanging upside down, barely attached, as though trying to remove itself out of embarrassment.

I knock and wait, the breeze from the river whipping tendrils of hair across my face, my hands being kept warm by the boxes of fish and chips I'm clutching to my chest, the smell making my stomach rumble in anticipation. I knock again, more loudly this time, expecting to hear movement within and a key turning in the lock any moment. It's just after 6pm, less than an hour before Aydan is due at mine, but it's unlikely he would have set off already as it's only a fifteen-minute journey. I frown and pull out my phone to check the message he sent again.

> Hey, AC, getting back to Hull around 5.30pm,
> so I'll shower, change and be at yours for 7pm.
> Shall we get a takeaway, my treat? A xxx

According to his text, I've timed my surprise visit perfectly, so where is he? Still in the shower? Although the thought of his soapy, naked body makes me smile, I'm sure he would have heard me knocking. I try once more and as if in forewarning, the upside-down number lands at my feet, finally having made its break for freedom. Perhaps I should leave now too, go home to Hardy sooner rather than later. I retreat to the warmth of my car to text my missing boyfriend.

Succumbing to the aroma of Hull's finest fish supper, I extract one of the polystyrene boxes and snaffle a few delicious, vinegary chips while I compose a message to Aydan. Afterwards, I stare absent-mindedly at the iron-grey view before me, pinpricks of light twinkling in the distance. It reminds me of the times in my previous life that I sat in a car alone with a worrying gut feeling, waiting for a man to make an appearance, to confirm what I hoped wasn't true.

An arc of headlights reflects in the rear-view mirror, and I watch as Aydan's car suddenly swings into view. He parks hastily on the kerb in front of his row of terraces. Relieved, I pick up the fish and chip boxes again, preparing to exit the car. I glance up just as he opens his door slightly, the interior light illuminating his face, but instead of getting out he stays in his seat, looking down into his lap. Perhaps he's about to text or ring me. I'm just about to leave the car to fulfil my plan – '*Surprise!*' – when my phone vibrates with a message, not a call.

> Paige I'm so sorry, there's been a huge
> emergency at work. It's not looking likely I'll get
> back tonight after all. Please say you'll agree to
> a rain check soon. Proper quality time? A xxx

I frown and look back up at the rear-view mirror to see Aydan slamming the car door shut and heading towards his house, except he doesn't go to the house I thought he lived at, he goes next door. I've been banging on the door of the wrong house! An assault of emotions delivers two quick, disorientating jabs: relief I got it wrong followed by the realisation that Aydan has just outright lied to me. Confused, I watch him disappear behind door number three and consider my options. I could confront him now or think things through. What on earth is he doing?

Before I even have the chance to decide and take any action, I see him come back out of the house again carrying a small holdall whilst also texting or dialling someone on his phone. I wait for another apologetic message to arrive, or my screen to light up with his call, but nothing happens. Our connection is severed. As he gets back in his car and speeds away, I can only watch his rear lights disappear, staring in shocked numbness until the food goes as cold as me. So much for Aydan being the one man who isn't acting suspiciously lately.

Arriving home a while later, the remains of the fish and chips deposited in a bin on Victoria Dock, Hardy greets me in his usual exuberant manner, his furry body deliciously warm on my cold hands. I pet him, grateful for his unwaning happy nature and his ability to make me smile despite everything that's going on.

My smile falters, however, as I see a trail of torn and chewed paper surrounding my desk and fanning out towards the dining table. Like breadcrumbs in a fairy story, I know they're going to lead to an unpleasant discovery. Sure enough, as I take a couple of steps forward, a now sorry-looking Hardy hanging back, I see pages and pages of my manuscript in tatters on the floor, a few escapees languishing on my chair after clearly being pulled off the desk.

'Hardy!' I cry, surging forward to inspect the damage, most of the A4 pages torn into an impossible confetti jigsaw, my now illegible red pen notes bleeding into the typed text. 'What's this?' I ask my naughty collie, pointing at the desecration of my hard work. He hangs his head in response, and I turn my face to the ceiling and close my eyes.

I know I can't be too mad at him – I left the hard copy out instead of putting it safely away in a drawer, but I didn't anticipate Hardy's separation anxiety to manifest itself in this way. Ever since we moved here and I began working from home, he's barely alone anymore and he's become a bit clingier, perhaps sensing that I need the company as much as he does.

I sigh heavily and kneel next to him, stroking his head and reassuring him it's okay. After my confusion and disappointment about James and now Aydan's outright lie, not to mention the anonymous text that still plays on my mind, I'm conscious that I'm trying to reassure myself too.

Chapter Eighteen

After a few unsettled and virtually hermit-like days worrying about Aydan's lie while painstakingly redoing my book edits following Hardy's manuscript attack, I'm looking forward to the respite of the writing group again this morning. Yet my stomach is in knots at the possibility of seeing James there. It's been over a week and a half since our date, and I haven't bumped into him while walking Hardy, even though I ventured out for our usual Westfield Park routine on Monday. The desire to see him again increased as soon as I sent a supposed breezy reply to my lying boyfriend, the guilt over my own deceit diminished in the wake of his blatant untruth.

Over the weekend Sylvie circulated an updated member email list to us all, so James has had an easy way of getting in touch with me since then, if he wanted to. Before that, he could have simply asked for my number. But he didn't. He obviously doesn't want to. Therefore, I must remember that my pride decided our cocktail bar encounter was a mistake *before* he ghosted me and *if* I see him today – his attendance record is non-existent after all – I'll be nothing more than perfectly polite and friendly. I don't want to jeopardise my place in the writing group over a silly crush, and after my outburst last week, Sylvie is probably already suspicious about whether I know him or not.

Aydan messaged again late last night, claiming the "emergency" had escalated, which meant he was working round the clock. He doubled down on his lie and repeated his apology for not being able to get home to spend the weekend together. I haven't responded to that one yet. I just don't know what to believe anymore.

According to the writing group rota, it should be Joy's turn to host our meeting but due to her ongoing renovation her house is still a building site, so she's been staying with her son. I've never been to Joy's, but I imagine it's full of exotic decoration – probably plenty of leopard print – amongst outrageous colour schemes and clashing patterns. I'm looking forward to seeing it when it's done. This week, Sylvie has kindly offered to hold the meeting at her house again, which will at least save her the bother of lugging her precious cafetière around the streets of Hull.

At exactly 10am, I'm the last to arrive in Sylvie's black-and-white-tiled outer porch, having taken more time than usual settling Hardy and leaving him with enough stimulation for a couple of hours, as well as doing a recce of the lounge diner and removing anything else he might be tempted to attack or destroy in my absence. I've also held off leaving until the last possible minute in an attempt to avoid any potential one-on-one interactions with James; safety in numbers and all that.

I nervously follow Sylvie into her beautiful open-plan kitchen, as overawed by the space as I was the first time I ever saw it. The bi-fold doors frame a multi-levelled, beautifully landscaped, large garden, and my gaze lingers over the impressive view, hesitant to register who is in the room and who isn't. But I already know James is here; I could sense him instantly.

Taking one of the two remaining empty seats, next to Joy, I fumble with my bag, extracting my notebook and pen whilst Sylvie brings the meeting to order. My peripheral vision acknowledges a steaming cup of coffee being pushed towards me and I force myself to glance across the table – at James. I offer a tight smile of thanks in return, grateful for the gesture yet more confused than ever – is this a peace offering, or has he shown everyone the same courtesy?

I force myself to focus on Sylvie as she outlines our two main agenda topics – the welcoming of James to the group, which she must have known about before today – followed by her repetition of the book fair arrangements, which by now we all know off by heart.

'Welcome, James!' She extends her arms to signify embracing his presence. 'It's wonderful to have you here – a fellow published author, I believe? How exciting!' Sylvie's exuberance does nothing to allay my anxiety. 'Shall we do quick introductions, everyone? Then we really must get on with business.'

In turn, we begin introducing ourselves to James. My heart threatens to combust with the exertion of its beating as, clasping my clammy hands together, I wait for the spotlight to swing my way. Do I let on that I know him? Do I pretend we are strangers? I opt for the latter, simply stating my name and how long I've been a member of the group whilst avoiding eye contact with anyone, especially him.

Once my extremely brief turn is over, I feel drained with the effort, but Sylvie swiftly moves the meeting on. If anyone is suspicious of my behaviour, I thankfully don't notice it. Despite her insistence on going through the book fair details for the hundredth time, everyone else seems to make a concerted effort to listen respectfully as Sylvie yet again parrots the running order of the day and the content of the workshop, but I can barely hear her words over the pounding of my heart. Still, I try my best to tune in.

'And as we are all aware, we also have – as a collective – secured a stall to spread the word about our group, as well as offer our books for sale. And by "our" I obviously mean the published authors among us. The stall needs to be manned *all* day, at *all* times, especially while I'm running the writing workshop in the adjoining hall, with Paige as my helper.' I wince at this pathetic description although I am grateful to not be up front and centre, exposed to the "huge crowds" that Sylvie goes on to state are "set to descend".

Joy throws me a smirk at the use of the hyperbolic phrasing but I look down, not only to spare Sylvie's feelings should she think we are mocking her exaggeration, but also to ensure I don't catch James's eye. I'm also feeling out of sorts at the thought of the book fair only being a few days away. I've managed to successfully stem my anxiety about it, until now, it seems, no doubt due to having more pressing issues to override it.

The remainder of the meeting passes quickly – only Joy reads her latest work to us today once the agenda topics have been ticked off (a shortish story about a burly Welsh trucker who legally changes his name to Pierrot Torreip to wriggle out of a complicated – and extremely confusing, if I'm honest – polyamorous situation gone very wrong). I chance at glance at Lloyd while she's reading and I'm sure he mouths the word 'tripe' at me with an 'I told you so' expression. I'm personally amazed by Joy's wild and vivid imagination and often wonder where she gets all her crazy ideas from.

Afterwards, we begin to disperse as Sylvie leads us to her front door vocalising the book fair bullet points yet again, as though she is a harassed teacher repeatedly reminding ignorant children of their responsibilities. I feel a pang of pity for her; she is clearly hanging her hopes on a few more sales of her book and

I know she will be so disappointed if there are none. I ridiculously consider corralling strangers in advance and giving them money to buy a couple of copies.

I hang back, the last to leave, waiting until everyone has gone ahead of me, for no other reason than to avoid any possible one-to-one contact with James. I consider nipping to the loo, but Sylvie is waiting expectantly by her grand entrance doors, eyes narrowed, probably at the prospect of me not leaving with everybody else and having to make conversation, just the two of us. It's not a prospect I fancy either; Sylvie is definitely an acquired taste, and I don't think I'm equipped to handle her caustic tongue alone.

'Bye, then, Sylvie. Thank you.' I wave awkwardly as I step over the threshold onto the front paved path, turning back to face her. 'See you at...' But she's already closed the door behind me, the ultimate full stop to the meeting. I sigh and dawdle my way off her property, giving the others even more time to get to their cars.

As I slowly meander out of Sylvie's driveway and along the tree-lined street towards my own car, waving to Joy as she drives by, tooting at me from her bright-yellow Cinquecento, I notice it. A gold Vauxhall Vectra. I stop and stare, convinced it's a figment of my imagination, but no, there it remains. I feel my heart rate pick up speed as my breathing becomes difficult.

No, no, it can't be, he can't be here.

My vision's too blurry to make out the number plate, part of which is obscured by the car parked behind it as well as one of the blossom trees starting to bloom prettily, and I pray for it not to be personalised. I bend, arms clasping my stomach, knees sinking down to the pavement, desperately gasping for air.

All at once I'm scooped up. James is at my side, one arm around my waist, steering me towards his waiting car, calming me, soothing me as I sob and shake. He opens the passenger door and guides me in, kneeling in front of me as my brain bursts with memories and my heart aches with regret and self-recriminations. I crane my neck to get a better look at the Vectra, furiously wiping my tears and forcing my eyes to focus, but they won't. James is watching me closely, his left hand on my knee. I push his hand off and stand up hurriedly, taking a few steps back from him.

'I'm okay, I'm okay,' I manage to splutter. 'I thought I saw someone I knew, that's all.'

'And it made you react like that? Are you sure you're okay, Paige?' He seems genuinely concerned. He approaches me and reaches out again, but I step away once more, repositioning my bag back on my shoulder and crossing my arms defensively. My fingers automatically seek the tender spot on my ribs, rubbing gently, trying to soothe myself.

'It was a silly panic attack. I'm fine now.' I refuse to meet his eyes as I wipe mine again and breathe deeply in an effort to restabilise myself.

'Do you have panic attacks often?' he asks.

I frown at him, at this intrusion, at this implied trust between us. 'That's really none of your business, is it?' I snap.

He holds his hands up in a placatory gesture, which only adds to the maelstrom of my internal storm.

'You seemed a little on edge at the meeting, I wanted to check it wasn't because of me, because of what happened...'

'What happened, exactly, James?' I bait, all thoughts of the Vectra and its possible occupant gone, the panicky feeling now morphing into anger. 'Are you referring to our sordid little snogging session despite my being in a relationship and you... you...' I don't even know how to end the sentence.

He frowns and looks down. 'Paige, I—'

'Save it,' I interrupt. 'I don't want to hear it. I've been a fool in the past but not this time.'

As I turn to leave, he grabs my arm. His grip is strong but I'm about to wrench myself free when he kisses me, hard, on the mouth. My eyes instantly close, muscle memory dictating my response despite my misgivings. He pulls away after a second or two and I don't move. When I open my eyes again, he is staring at me, slowly shaking his head.

'It wasn't sordid, Paige. Not for me,' he says in a low, secret tone before releasing me and turning back to his car.

As I watch him get in and drive off, I realise the gold Vectra has gone too, as though I imagined them both. I finally reach my own car and open the door with shaking fingers. Something catches my eye, and I glance back at Sylvie's house and catch sight of one of the upstairs net curtains falling back into place, or at least I think I do. Folding myself into the driver's seat, I lay my head on my arms on the steering wheel and wonder for a moment if I'm actually going mad.

Chapter Nineteen

The day of the book fair finally arrives, and I enter The Guildhall with plenty of time to help set up before the doors open at 9am. Getting up early wasn't a problem; I've barely slept since Wednesday following my panic attack in the street outside Sylvie's house after our writing group meeting. And although I've tried to put my insomnia to good use by working on my manuscript, immersing myself back into its oxymoronic reality fiction has only made my nerves even more twisted and badly frayed. It's a horribly familiar feeling.

What's happening lately? I thought I was back on an even keel, but all these reminders of the past are threatening to derail me again. But I can't let them, I've got to focus on the present. It's the only way to keep my sanity in check. I can't lose it again.

I spy Renee in the spacious lobby straight away. Interestingly, she appears to have roped her surly son Alexander into helping lug a few boxes of her books from the car to the hall, but he certainly doesn't look like he wants to be here. His scowl hasn't changed since the day I saw him on Renee's landing. I shudder slightly at the memory of his excessive fury.

The writer in me wonders what the story is there – Renee

has alluded to "trouble" and "chaos" a few times during our writing group meetings but she hasn't mentioned specifics. I smile at Alexander to convey no ill will on my part for his rudeness, but I'm rewarded with a hard expression for my trouble.

I hear Renee sigh as I approach her. 'Don't even bother with niceties, Paige,' she warns me as he passes by us and heads up the wide, blue-carpeted staircase. 'My darling son is not known for his friendliness.'

Inside, the main hall is already a bustle of activity in preparation for the fair opening in less than an hour. Tables are being positioned around the edges and in the centre of the room to create a meandering pathway around the array of soon-to-be stalls. Belinda has done a great job of organising a range of relevant small businesses to showcase their wares and I can't help but have a sneak peek at a few of them as I make my way over to the writing group's designated space. My eyes feast upon handmade cards featuring iconic book covers, to book-page art, to literary themed gifts being unpacked from bags, boxes and baskets, as well as a whole host of sweet and savoury food-based offerings from local bakers and small mobile kitchens.

The atmosphere is industrious and quite exciting, and I feel slightly foolish for being worried about it; absolutely nobody is paying attention to me – after all, why on earth would they? I've made blending into the background an art form.

I spot Belinda circulating with her clipboard, issuing instructions to other stallholders in her usual efficient manner, as well as Kenny and Lloyd chatting by the tea and coffee urns at the back, getting their priorities right.

Sylvie is already unloading her own stack of books and arranging them front and centre of our stall, with no regard for the placement of anyone else's. Standard Sylvie. She is clearly in author mode, dead set on marketing and promotion. I'm mentally crossing my fingers that she sells a few books, if only to bolster her ego and ensure she's pleasantly buoyed rather than snarky and bitter when interacting with the few writing workshop sign-ups we've got. There are ten confirmed, a perfectly manageable number for Sylvie, but I definitely cannot face them by myself, especially not today when I'm still feeling so fragile

Trying to shake myself out of it and focus on the fair, I quickly stow my bag under the display table with Sylvie's boxes. I've brought my partially re-annotated manuscript with me so I can reward myself with an hour of focused work in Hull's central library around the corner once I've done my bit here. After being surrounded by people for half the day, the introvert in me will need a quiet space to recharge as well as hopefully borrow a few books I've got on my TBR pile and return the editing books I've borrowed, before getting home to Hardy, who I've forgiven for using my first manuscript as a chew toy, but who I don't trust alone in the house with its replacement. Aydan claims he's working again this weekend too – whether that's true or not remains a mystery but at least I'll have books to keep me company. A novel is often a better option than a man anyway.

I bend down to reach for a few of Renee's books from one of the boxes Alexander has just plonked on the floor, to display alongside Sylvie's, and as I do someone bumps into me from behind. I hear an exclaimed apology as I turn around. It's James. I can feel my face immediately redden, and I notice Sylvie stealing sticky beak glances at us within my peripheral vision.

'Hello, Paige,' he says softly, no doubt fully aware of Sylvie's prying eyes too. 'Can I help?' He gestures to the boxes of books at our feet, eyebrows raised, waiting for my response.

'Sure,' I reply, curtly. 'These books need unpacking and displaying. I'll go and check if Renee needs anything else bringing in.'

I make a hasty escape and on my way down to the foyer, I run into Joy, who is laden down too. Behind her in the car park opposite, Renee is talking to, or rather at, a pouting Alexander, who looks more like a precocious little boy than a strapping adult man, especially with his hood up against the fine drizzle now falling. I decide to keep my distance.

'Darling! How are you?' Joy effuses, puffing from the weight of two bulging canvas bags. 'You couldn't possibly take one of these, could you? I'm jiggered!'

I laugh at her turn of phrase while relieving her of one of the bags which is full of books. I glance inside and spy a familiar title. 'What's this?' I ask, surprised.

'I've been a sneaky little thing, Paige.' She giggles girlishly as she reaches into the bag. 'I've only gone and published a few copies of the first book in my series with help from that lovely cover designer Madeleine that Sylvie seems to have already seen off! I thought I could shift a few here today, give Sylvie a bit of competition!' She holds up a paperback with one of the most amateur-looking – and bordering on inappropriate – covers I've ever seen.

'But they've not been fully edited or proofread yet, Joy,' I counter, now equally concerned about the interior and exterior of the books.

'Oh, that doesn't matter, darling – Madeleine says that readers of books like these are willing to overlook a few typos to get their spicy fix! I thought I'd test that theory today, drum up a bit of interest and sell these as draft copies at a reduced price. Now, don't be such a sourpuss and help me get them centre of attention on the stall.' She seems very pleased with herself, and I don't have the heart to tell her that this isn't really how it's done, and all she risks drumming up is a lot of negative feedback from any hardcore erotic fiction fans out there.

But who am I to tell Joy what she can and can't do? I'm sure

Sylvie will give her opinion freely enough, however, any stall tension could impact negatively on Sylvie's mood and inclination to run the workshop. The last thing I need is for her to cry off, leaving it all to me, in favour of competing with Renee and now Joy in the book showcasing stakes.

As I dutifully follow Joy back into the main hall, my own mood turns greyer at the prospect of an already difficult day now becoming an unbearable one, but I can't let anyone down. I promised I would be here, so here I must stay, despite my increasing anxiety.

At 9am, the book fair officially opens and members of the public start to stream steadily into the space, holding still-dripping umbrellas, wiping wet glasses and shaking the rain off their hair and coats. There are more than I expected considering the drizzle has become a downpour and I'm pleased to have other people to focus on. Sylvie's reaction to Joy not only now being a newly published author but also impeaching on her display space with her "lurid" books, has already created quite the strained atmosphere, as I anticipated. Joy either genuinely hasn't noticed or genuinely doesn't care as she presents her book to passers-by like a perfume spritzer in a department store, actually making a few instant sales (and possibly fans), whilst Sylvie's sour expression turns more and more murderous.

Add to the mixture an extremely harassed Renee, a furious-looking Alexander who appears to have been forced to stay in the seat next to his mother, a bitter Lloyd because his traditionally published books aren't featured at all, an affable Kenny who keeps getting in everyone's way, and a strangely brooding James, and I can't help but feel it's all turning out to be a recipe for disaster.

Chapter Twenty

I'm counting down the minutes until our writing workshop because I have every intention of leaving as soon as it has finished, and I have fulfilled my duties as Sylvie's "helper". I'm now desperate to head straight to the central library in Albion Street to re-edit a few more chapters of my manuscript without distraction.

Of course, I know I should have been updating the digital version as I went, but there's something special about putting pen to actual paper and striking through words and sentences with red pen, making notes in margins and peppering paragraphs with arrows and asterisks and question marks, especially when I'm so connected to the text itself. And once I've finished editing the hard copy as methodically and as meticulously as I can, then I'll make the necessary changes on my laptop before emailing it to Lloyd's editor contact. I'm so nearly there now, even after Hardy's unexpected intervention. It'll feel so strange to let the story go, but I must if I'm ever going to properly sever myself from that horrific time of my life. Freeing it means freeing myself from its hold over me.

As 11am approaches, I inform Sylvie that I'm going to set

up the workshop in the smaller adjoining hall and wander through to the space, grateful for the peace and quiet. It may only be classed a local fair, but it is in the UK's City of Culture and Belinda's done a great job on the advertising front as it already seems to be a roaring success. The hubbub from the main hall carries through like a song on the radio.

As I'm moving a few wobbly tables and positioning padded metal folding chairs in preparation for the workshop's attendees, I realise I've forgotten to collect Sylvie's box of resources from under the group's stall and quickly head back to retrieve it. It appears one of the others is one step ahead of me though as Alexander is standing in the doorway, holding the box I need. His coat is still on, as though ready to leave at any moment, yet he hasn't. He's been rooted to his chair all morning like a reprimanded detainee. He doesn't say anything, just stares at me, like a stunning sculpted statue.

'Is that for me?' I force myself to ask chirpily, trying to appear less ruffled than I feel, holding out my arms ready to accept the box.

His eyes narrow. 'What has she told you about me?' he asks, clutching the box to his chest instead of passing it to me, the anger emanating from him like smoke, as though he's burning within.

'Who?' For a moment I am genuinely perplexed by the unexpected question as much as the strange encounter itself.

'Her – Renee,' he spits the name out, disgust evident on his face.

I'm bewildered for a moment. 'Your mum?' I ask.

He makes a sound that may be an attempt at a mirthless laugh, but I can't be sure. His face is twisted, an ugly expression on such a flawless canvas. His eyes flash with hatred. 'She's a fucking liar.' He drops the resources box clumsily onto a nearby chair rather than hand it over to me, spins on his heel and stalks off back to the main hall.

I'm rattled and confused and have no idea how to react to this bizarre exchange – whether to speak to Renee, whether to tell anyone else about it, or whether to simply focus on the job in hand and continue preparing for the workshop, which will either take my mind off it, or merely keep my hands busy while I try to make sense of it.

I can feel myself withdrawing, slipping back into myself, my overactive brain registering conflict and confusion everywhere, seeing slyness and suspecting secrets. It's becoming too much. I sit down on the chair next to the resources box and try to calm myself down. I can't have another panic attack here, not now.

Somehow, I get through the hour-long workshop, having decided to remain tight-lipped about Alexander's odd behaviour. Only nine people turned up in the end – all over seventy by the looks of them. Sylvie, seemingly grateful for the stall book war rather than territorial about it now that she's managed to sell a few copies, regales the captive attendees with her self-publishing story instead of sticking to our pre-agreed writing prompts and exercises.

Thankfully, she is very well received by the suitably impressed few and when Belinda pops in just before 12pm to see how the workshop has gone, I take the opportunity to sneak back through to the main hall to collect my bag, intending to say a quick goodbye to everyone so that I am free to leave and escape to the safety of the library as soon as the workshop is done.

As I re-enter the hall, I see that Renee and Joy are still happily marketing their books to a small gathering of people, and that they appear to have sold plenty between them, if the dwindling piles on the stall are anything to go by. I'm pleased for them both, and for Sylvie, as well as relieved that I can flee in the next few minutes.

Alexander's seat is now empty, Kenny is nowhere to be seen, and James and Lloyd are in conversation over by the tea and coffee station. Although I don't want to do anything to bring attention to myself, I don't want to be rude either, so I quickly wave in their direction as I head straight for the stall. James's gaze follows me, but I determinedly don't acknowledge it. I've managed to avoid speaking to him properly by keeping my focus on fair attendees for the whole morning. It's completely drained my social battery but rather that than endure another embarrassing or awkward exchange, in public this time.

As Renee and Joy are in full flow sales mode with their small crowd, I surreptitiously crouch down behind the stall to collect my bag so that I don't interrupt them. I can hear their conversations and they're doing a brilliant job of promoting their books. Joy's tinkling laugh has been a soundtrack to her success today. Except for taking a call from her son earlier, she's been steadfastly stuck to the stall, selling, selling, selling. I admire her doggedly determined and entrepreneurial approach to her books. I wish I could be more like her.

My hand flounders below the table, amongst the empty boxes, reaching for my bag. I've got one eye on James while I grope around, praying he doesn't come over, panic beginning to rise as I feel nothing but cardboard and polished parquet flooring. As I kneel forward to check properly, I already know for certain that it's not there, but I methodically tip all the boxes upside down anyway, in a fruitless attempt to locate my bag, and more importantly, my manuscript.

I can sense Renee and Joy and the small gathering watching me as I become more and more flustered, now on my hands and knees under the table, frantically glancing all around me for my bag's familiar floral handle.

Renee leans down, concern etched on her face. 'Paige, are you okay under there? What's wrong?'

More feet appear in my eyeline, and I realise that James and Lloyd have been alerted to my distress too.

'My bag,' I cry, shaking. 'My bag's gone... it had my manuscript inside... someone's stolen it!'

'What?' she says, crouching down next to me. 'Are you sure you left it here?'

'Of course I'm sure! You must have seen someone take it – it was right here!' I shout, completely beside myself. It feels as though everyone in the hall is looking at me, their eyes full of pity for the pathetic, panic-stricken girl. Sounds become muffled as the walls of the hall seem to shift around me like a terrifying optical illusion. I kneel, arms wrapped around myself, rocking backwards and forwards, while everyone stares.

Chapter Twenty-One

On Monday morning I force myself to leave the house to meet Joy. The weak spring sunshine is a shock to my red-rimmed eyes after being holed up in the house for the remainder of the weekend, throwing myself a pity party. Hardy sensed my sadness and stayed curled up next to me, offering his unique and very welcome version of support.

I even refused Aydan's many calls and subsequent texts suggesting a FaceTime chat. He claimed he wanted to hear all about the success of the book fair, and I claimed I had a sudden mystery illness and couldn't even muster up the energy to speak. Not that I wanted to tell him what had happened, not after he's broken my trust with his bare-faced lie about still being at work in Scotland when he was actually here, in Hull, when I was outside his house. But wallowing in grief for the loss of my revised and re-annotated manuscript for the second time, and fury at my own stupidity for leaving it unattended at the book fair made for a very lonely and miserable day and a half. Although I do have the original extremely rough draft on my laptop, it's still hours and hours of editing gone to waste – again. Not to mention the fact that I haven't anonymised names yet, including my own, though thankfully I've mostly only used "her" and "him" throughout for myself and he-who-I-don't-really-want-to-name.

Belinda was brilliant on Saturday, immediately announcing the theft of my bag. Judging by some of the looks thrown my way I'm sure some people thought I had simply misplaced it and was overreacting. Belinda encouraged a thorough search of the halls, and the lobby, but to no avail. Renee, Joy and James tried their best to calm me down, even Sylvie, Kenny and Lloyd seemed empathetic, despite their apparent inclination for preferring practical solutions rather than placating rising hysteria.

After an hour of looking under every table in the hall as well as frantically retracing my steps around the entire building, even though I knew I had stowed it safely upon arrival, I had to leave. I pinned my fading hopes on Belinda's promise to ring me if anyone located my bag after I had gone, thankful for the small mercy of keeping my phone, my bank card and my house key in my coat pocket.

As I rushed out of the hall, desperately trying to stem fresh tears, James caught up with me. He held my arms and turned me to face his imploring blue eyes.

'Paige, let me drive you home. You're in no fit state. Please, talk to me, let me help you.'

'Leave me alone!' I raged, wild-eyed and defiant, embarrassed he was seeing me in such a mess twice in the same week. 'Just leave me alone!'

With impeccable timing, his mobile rang. Freezing for a split second, I could see him mentally deliberating whether to allow the intrusion. He checked the caller display, tutted, sagged and whispered, 'I'm so sorry, I've got to answer this.'

I shook my head at his decision, thoughts of the caller being the mysterious Sofia invading my brain, gatecrashing in beside my resident mental anguish, then I broke free of his hold, ran across the road to my car, and sobbed my heart out once inside. I'd barely stopped crying until I fell asleep last night.

Joy and Renee both emailed yesterday to check how I was, and I acquiesced to seeing Joy this morning, in the hope that she will work her cheerful magic and help yank me out of this terrible slump I've found myself in.

As Joy's house is still being held hostage by builders and I need a change of scenery, we have agreed to meet at our newly preferred coffee shop in Anlaby. Joy's late, as always, so I nurse my latte at a table in the window for a few minutes while I wait. My mind is in turmoil, yet again going over everything, and I feel another stab of sadness at losing my favourite photo of my parents which was inside my purse in my bag. It was the anniversary of their deaths yesterday, which felt excruciatingly poignant. Twenty years without them now and I still feel like that lost little twelve-year-old girl most of the time. I'll have fines to pay for the loss of the library books that were taken too. Books and memories are all that I had and now I feel as though I don't even have those. It's just all too much to cope with.

I make a list on my phone to try to order my messy thoughts:

- *Mysterious text message – who could have sent it, and why?*
- *Aydan lied to me – claimed to be working overtime but went home (next door?)*
- *Vauxhall Vectra outside Sylvie's – was it him?*
- *James kissed me twice despite me being with Aydan and him getting calls from Sofia – no contact in the interim*
- *Alexander behaving strangely and aggressively – accused Renee of being a liar*

> • *My bag (containing my manuscript) stolen at book fair – was it a deliberate or a chance theft?*

'Cooee, darling!' Joy appears at my side, startling me, which isn't difficult in my permanently anxious state. I offer up a shaky smile as she air-kisses both cheeks, her heavy perfume wafting around me. I'm grateful for her usual exuberance and immediately pleased that I've ventured out to see her. She always seems to know when I need a bit of a bolster.

As Joy flutters about ordering and being overly interested in the barista – 'Everyone is a potential character, don't you know!' – I quickly close my list and check my messages. Lloyd has emailed, apologetically chasing a proofreading progress report on his manuscript, newly positive after witnessing the other members' successful book fair sales despite his scathing opinion of their talents, and I squirm in my seat. I've barely glanced at it recently with everything else going on. I quickly email him back, promising I'll update him at our next group meeting on Wednesday.

I place my phone on the table as Joy finally joins me, her flirty laughter lingering as the barista wryly smiles after her. She's like magic; able to cast a spell on everyone she meets.

'Now, Paige, my love, what the dickens is going on with you lately?' Joy comes straight to the point in her kind yet forthright manner. 'I must confess we're all a bit worried about you, especially after what happened on Saturday. Why don't you tell Auntie Joy what's wrong?'

'Who's worried? What are they saying?' I ask, picking anxiously at my dry lips.

Joy pouts her red smudged lips as she stirs her drink, clearly considering whether to share the information she holds. She doesn't consider for long.

'Well, it's Sylvie.' She leans forward and places her long-fingernailed hand on my arm. The contact reminds me of when I first met Aydan in Starbucks, and I blink the thought away. 'Now, don't shoot the messenger but she claims she saw you and the new boy James in a tryst in the street after last week's meeting! Joy sits back again, heavily pencilled eyebrows raised questioningly at this piece of information. I blush instantly.

'A tryst?' I look away and consider forcing a laugh, trying to make the idea seem ludicrous along with the old-fashioned word itself, but I know I'm as transparent as the window we're sitting beside.

She studies me for a moment as I take a sip of lukewarm coffee and attempt to compose myself into someone believable, but she's still not fooled. She leans forward again, hand back on my arm. 'Be careful there, darling,' she warns. 'Aren't you already seeing a young fellow?'

I feel caught out and ashamed and I notice my hands are shaking as they cradle my cup. Whatever must Joy think of me? What must they all think of me? I thought I'd been doing so well in leaving these feelings of shame and inadequacy behind me, but they've followed me here, too. Tears well in my eyes and one spills over into my latte with a tiny splash.

'Oh, dear girl, come on now.' Joy clucks her tongue, handing me her serviette. 'What's got you this upset? Has Sylvie got it terribly wrong? Is she mixing you up with one of her fairy-tale fantasy characters in her books?'

I shake my head and look up at her with watery eyes. 'No, that's just it, she did see us in the street – I thought she did at the time – but it wasn't a "tryst" as she calls it.'

Joy waits patiently for me to continue, giving me her full attention.

I take a deep breath. 'I had a panic attack and James helped me then he kissed me. It wasn't a mutual kiss... not that time anyway,' I whisper.

'So, you two are engaged in a dalliance of sorts?' she asks.

I shrug. 'I think so but it's so weird. There's definitely something between us but I've already made it clear it's a mistake to pursue it. I thought he thought that too and backed off but...'

'But what, Paige?' prompts Joy, her dark brows furrowed, her black-rimmed eyes full of concern.

'I don't know for sure. I think he might already have a wife or girlfriend – called Sofia – and he knows I'm already with someone... he's called Aydan. But James is so kind to me. Aydan works away so he's barely here and what with everything else going on...' I press my lips together and shake my head. I feel so pathetic, so ill equipped to deal with life, never mind potential love.

'Darling, what do you mean by "everything else going on"?' Joy picks up her cup, watching me beadily over the rim as she takes a drink.

I falter for a moment, my mind swirling through the list on my phone, reluctant to share my worries and paint myself as even more of a crazy person. My writing group has been my anchor, a steadfast beacon of possibility that people and the world are inherently good, despite years of evidence to the contrary. I'm loath to do, or say, anything that might jeopardise that. I realise sadly, however, that I may already have. I decide to trust Joy and show her my list.

Over the next hour and another coffee each, I go through the points in turn. However, I gloss over the Vectra sighting somewhat, wary about opening that Pandora's box of questions, instead giving Joy the basic facts but not the full picture. I think she is beginning to understand why I've been so jumpy lately. I needn't have worried; she is a paragon of sympathy, and my relief is immense.

'Oh, you poor thing, my love.' She shakes her head at me, her expression full of sympathy. 'You've had quite a bit to cope with, haven't you? Not that I condone cheating or altercations with taken men, but I know from personal experience how persuasive they can be when they want something, or someone.'

'You've been involved with a married man?' I ask. I have no right to be shocked although I am a bit. I don't really know anything about Joy's romantic situation, other than I think she once mentioned that she got divorced many years ago. I've often seen her on her phone lately – perhaps there's a new man on the scene? If so, good for her.

'No, quite the opposite, in fact,' she replies. 'My husband was the persuasive one and off he went with the object of his desire – a younger model, obviously. Some men have no imagination.' She tuts and shakes her head, her hair-sprayed nest of hair staying in place. 'Not even a backward glance at me. Not seen hide nor hair of the cheating rotter since.'

I gasp. Oh, Joy, I'm so sorry.'

She waves a hand as if to bat away the sympathy before it can settle on her. 'It's not something I broadcast, obviously, but he was a charming lothario who, unfortunately, charmed me along the way too. He did me one favour though – well, apart from fathering my brilliant son, I will give him that – he provided great cannon fodder for the dastardly bastards in my books!'

Despite everything, I laugh and I'm grateful for her light-heartedness which counteracts my misery. I already feel more positive and determined to figure everything out, even if that does mean confronting both my past and my present before I can really move on.

As Joy and I say our goodbyes, with her using her standard

phrase of 'See you soon, darling, toodle-pip!' and I thank her once again for her support, my phone buzzes with a text. It's from Aydan.

> Hey, AC, missing you madly. I'm so sorry again for being MIA lately. You, me, lunch out on Saturday, how about it? A xxx

Despite everything that's happened lately, I allow myself to feel a tentative flutter of hope. Perhaps some things are going to be all right.

What's Happened to You?

Six months to the day after their engagement, she ventured out to watch and revel in the ordinariness she wished she still experienced.

'What's happened to you?' Julia asked her, taking in the pale face, greasy hair and naked nails, a look so at odds with the attractive and carefully coiffed young woman she had met in the newspaper offices a few years before. She had watched her friend slowly decline in the weeks before her departure, but the sight before her now was nothing short of shocking.

Her face crumpled at her old friend and colleague's concern, shame reddening her cheeks as she realised how badly she had withered since she had been asked to leave her old job, one she revelled in and was excellent at. She could still remember her manager's expression of disappointment and distaste during her exit interview. It haunted her.

'Come on now.' Julia scooted her chair nearer, proffering the flimsy serviette from her cup of tea and resting her chin on her hand, the journalist in her patiently waiting for a response – never force the conversation, let them talk in their own time.

'It's all such a mess,' she said, anguished, eyes wide and full of emotion, spinning the engagement ring she had grown to hate round her slender finger. Every time she looked at it she felt a bewildering conflict of emotions. Mainly sadness.

Julia the journalist, desperate for a pen, noted the fear in her friend's expression and nodded encouragingly yet sympathetically, she hoped. This might have the makings of a story. She might finally be able to help her.

— *Descent into Deceit*

Chapter Twenty-Two

The last time I set eyes on Aydan was the brief secret sighting of him that night outside his house two weeks ago. After a lot of thought, I've decided not to mention it today. I don't want to spoil our reunion lunch with stalker-like suspicions, especially when I've got secrets of my own. Talk about pot calling the kettle black.

After my confessional with Joy on Monday, I've been feeling much better about everything. I'm regaining a normal perspective again, and I've successfully maintained my distance from James after deciding – for the first time since I joined – to skip the writing group meeting on Wednesday just gone. I didn't give Joy permission to share my problems, but I trust that she tactfully batted away any questions about me following my scene at the book fair, especially from Sylvie. I just need a bit of time until I feel emotionally equipped enough to face everyone again. Yes, my manuscript being stolen is absolutely devastating to me, considering the amount of work I had already done on it – twice – but I can print it off and start yet again, so all is not completely lost following the theft and my subsequent panic attack. Except my time, my pride and perhaps a bit of my sanity.

But I'm trying to learn patience – to take a step back before reacting, to focus on the positives.

Speaking of positives, I'm early to the newly opened café in Hull's old town near Trinity Church but, to my surprise, Aydan's already here. I'm taken aback by how great he looks, even better than the first time I ever met him. He's dressed in dark-blue jeans and an olive-green shirt, coordinating beautifully with the soothing blues and greens of the café's décor, his colourful tattoos adding an edge.

I've made an effort too. All my worries of late have resulted in me dropping another few pounds so I've worn a colourful pleated skirt paired with a thin black jumper and small heels. Aydan's expression shows me he approves and although I still have my suspicions about him, I feel terrible about my own recent behaviour too. Surely two wrongs cancel each other out? I once again chastise myself that my head could be so easily turned by James and vow here and now to rectify it.

'Hi, beautiful.' He stands and kisses me firmly on the mouth, one hand lightly on my waist. 'I'm pleased you're feeling better, it's so good to see you.' He pulls the chair next to his out for me.

'You too,' I reply as I sit down at the window table he has chosen for us, knowing my preference for being able to see the comings and goings in any public place, even if he doesn't know the reason behind it. I've been very careful not to divulge too much about my reasons for moving here so far and he's hardly questioned me about it at all, as though he understands that everyone has a past they'd rather not dredge up. He's become a bit of a closed book too but at least we're even on that score, and it doesn't have to mean we can't enjoy the time we do spend together.

He takes one of my hands in his. 'I'm so sorry it's been so

long since we've seen each other, Paige. Work's been crazy and–'

'It's okay,' I interrupt, reassuring him, placing my other hand over his and leaning towards him. 'We're here together now, no apologies necessary.'

He looks at me for a moment as though he's wondering whether to disagree but whatever's going on behind the scenes of his gaze disappears, quickly replaced with gratitude, I think. I hope. It's not fair if he apologises to me when I realise now that I'm more in the wrong for kissing another man behind his back.

Our meals are simple and delicious, and as we eat, I fill Aydan in on what's been happening in my life while he's been away, albeit a rather patchy version. I tell him about my two encounters with Renee's son Alexander and about my manuscript going missing at the book fair. Aydan immediately puts two and two together and announces that Alexander is the culprit.

'Do you think he could be?' I ask, surprised the answer could be that simple.

'Sounds like it to me, Paige. He's unnerved you twice then was nowhere to be seen when you went to collect your bag. You know all your writing group friends wouldn't have taken it and he had access to it all day.'

'But why would he do that? What's his motive?'

He grins. 'Such a classic Agatha Christie response. Sometimes there is no clear motive. It sounds like he's got a screw loose. If he hates his mum maybe he wanted to cause trouble for her in some way? Or maybe he just wanted to cause trouble full stop, for his own amusement?'

I frown, thinking about the fierce – and definitely not amused – look on Alexander's face at the book fair, and the way he carelessly dumped the box of resources onto the chair. Is that enough evidence to label him a deliberate thief? Aydan seems to think so.

'So, say he is the number one suspect, what should I do about it, if anything? I can't just accuse him, and I really don't want to insult Renee in any way.'

'Did you check outside the town hall? If he took your bag out of pure devilment, he might have just chucked it once he realised there wasn't much of value in it. Not that your manuscript isn't valuable,' he quickly corrects himself, flashing me another smile.

'Yes, as far as I know someone checked outside, but I don't know how carefully so that could be a possibility,' I agree, belated hope blooming in my chest that my possessions could be recovered.

'You could check Renee's house too, see if he's stashed it there.'

'I can't do that, it's snooping!' I playfully tap him on the arm, and he laughs.

'You're too honest for your own good, Paige Carrigan,' he replies.

I look back down at my plate and hope he never realises that honest is something I'm definitely not.

A short while later I'm wondering whether to suggest ordering another drink and settling here for a little while longer when Aydan's phone rings. He groans, frowning as he pulls it from the pocket of his jeans.

'No way, I don't believe this!' he exclaims. I assume it's his work calling, and I tell him to take it, that I don't mind, although today I actually do. We're having such a nice time.

He apologises as he goes outside to take the call and I watch him pace back and forth outside the window, running his fingers through his styled hair and shaking his head. I can't help but think back to the lie he told that night outside his house again, and find myself wondering if it is his work or something – or perhaps someone – else. Maybe it's all a performance to make sure he spends less time with me. I chuckle softly at my own thoughts; I swear sometimes my own brain is out to get me.

After a few minutes he returns to me, scowling, ramming his phone back in his pocket. His face says it all.

'You've got to go back early, haven't you?' I save him having to explain.

'I just wanted one weekend off. I thought it was sorted but they need me there tonight. It's a good job I haven't had more than one drink.' He looks furious and suddenly extremely tired, no doubt anticipating the long journey ahead that he made only late last night.

'You go, I'll take care of the bill,' I offer as he snatches up his jacket and shrugs it on. He opens his mouth to object but I'm already out of my seat. 'Let me,' I say firmly, keen to do something to salve my own conscience.

After I've settled the bill, I offer to walk with him to his car and he responds by taking my hand and giving it a squeeze.

'I parked in the multi-storey as I had a few errands to run earlier. It's right across town so I'd better leg it and nip home for my work stuff. You go on and I'll call you later tonight, once I'm there.'

He kisses me briefly but forcefully in the doorway of the café, as we shelter from an overcast sky threatening rain, quite aptly given the now miserable circumstances. I try not to think of the last time I was kissed in a doorway but the memory of that night with James pops into my mind regardless. Will I ever stop thinking about it – the tenderness of it? Despite his roughness, I attempt to kiss Aydan again in an effort to bring my thoughts back on track but he's already snapping his collar up, cushioning his beard against the wind. He winks at me and smiles instead, then he's gone, and I'm left shivering, alone, wondering whether he's really going back to Scotland or not.

Chapter Twenty-Three

It's Wednesday again and it's my turn to host the writing group. It'll be the first time I've seen everyone since the book fair and I'm unsure how to play it – overtly tough or apologetic for my "crazy" behaviour? Although I feel better having spoken to Joy and enough time has passed that I'm beginning to feel on a bit more of an even keel, I'm still anxious about everything that happened that day. Should I mention Alexander's remarks to Renee? Should I talk to James and get everything out in the open so we can potentially move forward as friends? Should I be suspicious of all of them or could Alexander really be the one who took my bag and manuscript, as Aydan suggested he did? These thoughts have been flying around my brain for days, swooping down to peck at me frequently.

As people begin to arrive and I bustle about in the kitchen, I decide I'm going to address it at the start of the meeting and get it out of the way in the hope that it'll make things not weird. Or not *as* weird. As I'm making the coffees, having already acquired the cafetière from a surprisingly smiley Sylvie, Lloyd appears in the doorway.

'Paige, can I have a word?'

I'm instantly nervous. I know this is going to be about his manuscript because I've taken far too long proofreading it. I feel a wash of shame; it's not professional – he's a client now, I still have my reputation to consider, and this project could potentially lead to more paying clients in the future.

'I just wanted to say about my manuscript—'

'Lloyd, I'm so sorry for the delay,' I interrupt him, neglecting the refreshments to give him my full attention. 'It's no excuse, but with everything that's been going on lately—'

It's his turn to interrupt. He holds up a hand, shaking his head. 'It's okay, you don't have to explain, I know things have been tough for you so please just invoice me for the work you've already done. I think I'm going to turn it over to a professional.' His tone isn't malicious, but it still stings like an unexpected paper cut.

'Professional?' I repeat as a shame-induced heat reaches the surface of my skin.

'I don't mean you're not professional, of course not,' he says, immediately backtracking. 'I just mean in the industry proper. I'm finally going to bite the bullet and ask a contact of a contact to appraise it for me. I've had enough of hiding bitterly in the background.' He glances over his shoulder, lowering his voice. 'If the likes of Joy and Sylvie can sell boxes of their mediocre fairy tale and fuck-fest stories at a local book fair, I should be able to at least get an opinion on mine from someone who really knows their stuff.' He chuckles nastily and I'm taken aback. 'I should thank them really, for spurring me into action. Anyway, you don't need to worry about it anymore, you've got enough on your plate.'

What does Lloyd actually know about what's on my plate? He's implying I've bitten off more than I can chew with my business – that I'm not a proficient proofreader. I stare at him, offended for a moment, considering whether to try to change the mind of a man whose words imply that he doesn't respect anyone in the group anyway. And then I see the pity in his eyes. He thinks I'm not fit for purpose since the book fair. I drop my gaze, instantly embarrassed and ashamed rather than indignant; I've made a mess of this.

'I understand,' I say quietly. 'I'll invoice you. Would you please carry the tray of cups through for me?'

He nods and does as I ask, leaving me alone in the kitchen, reeling. I open the back door to let Hardy out, taking a few deep breaths of fresh air, willing myself not to cry. I haven't even explained my last emotional outburst yet; it's too soon for another.

A few minutes later, as soon as we've all taken our places in my small living room, I jump straight in, eager to get it all off my chest, before Sylvie has a chance to start on the agenda. I'm sitting as far away from James as I can and I don't look directly at anyone as I speak, fearful of seeing sympathy – or worse – in their eyes, which will certainly make me lose my nerve and shed more tears. Poor, deranged Paige. No, I need to show I've got some semblance of control here, before I risk losing everyone's respect and my place in the group completely.

'I just wanted to quickly say thank you, everyone, for helping me look for my missing bag and manuscript at the book fair and I'm sorry if any of you felt I had accused you of stealing them. I've been going through a bit of a stressful time lately and it really was the last straw that day. I know I haven't known you for very long in the grand scheme of things, but I do trust you all and I know none of you would have done anything so devious. It obviously got picked up by accident and my overactive writer's imagination thought the worst. So, again, I'm sorry for what I said, I'm sorry for how I reacted and I'm sorry for any fuss I caused.'

'No apologies necessary, darling,' responds Joy straight away, with everyone else nodding along and adding their reassurances too, which ironically makes me feel quite emotional. I chance a quick glance at them all and nobody seems to be wearing anything but a concerned expression, even Sylvie. James smiles warmly at me and I'm happy he's here, despite our strange and strained relationship.

The rest of the meeting passes without any more drama. Joy shares her ideas for another far-fetched erotic romance novel she is planning which instantly lightens the mood and subsequently my spirits, despite Lloyd rolling his eyes while she's talking, and Kenny reads a short story he has written. It's the first time I've ever heard Kenny share anything and I'm pleasantly surprised at his writing talent. It's true, it seems, the quieter writers are often the most observant and intuitive.

On my way back downstairs after popping to the loo, I hear my name and I realise the group are talking about me – here in my own house. I can't hear everything, but a few snatches are clear enough:

'...unstable for a while...'

'...mortified for her, poor thing...'

I sink down to sit on the step, knees pulled up to my chest. I'm a hot gossip topic and I burn with the shame of it. A couple of minutes later, after I've managed to compose myself, I return to the living room. A hush immediately descends, and Sylvie has the grace to look embarrassed. I don't let on that I heard them.

The meeting draws to a close and Sylvie, Lloyd and Kenny are the first to leave. James hangs back as Joy steps outside, throwing a raised eyebrow over her shoulder as she wiggles her fingers in a goodbye. Embarrassed, I say goodbye to him and attempt to make a move to close the door. He stops it with a firm hand.

'Can we talk please, Paige?'

'What about?' I ask obtusely, my wall of defence sky high now, built back up after being dropped by Lloyd and hearing my supposed friends gossiping about me.

'Us. Whatever this is,' he says, signalling backwards and forwards between us with his finger.

'There is no us.' I mirror his movement.

'I think there is, there can be.'

The tears come then, bubbling up suddenly from within me, and he instantly moves closer. I let him wipe them away with both thumbs, then cup my face in his hands as even more overflow. If he kisses me now, I know I won't be able to resist, despite all my good intentions. A voice from the past whispers in my ear, telling me I'm nothing but a whore, desperate for attention from any man that shows even the slightest bit of interest, thirstily gulping down any compliment, any affection whatsoever. I screw my eyes shut, trying to block the voice out and yet more tears spill over onto James's hands, but he doesn't move them away. I shake my head furiously.

'No, no...'

'Paige, I can't stop thinking about you, and I–'

'You what?' I shout, surprising us both, knocking his hands away forcefully and taking a small step back within the confines of my narrow hallway. 'You want me? You didn't want me enough to try to contact me after our night in the cocktail bar, or anytime since then. And what about Sofia – who is she to you?' I ask boldly.

He shakes his head. 'Sofia... it's complicated.'

'It's complicated for me too. I'm with Aydan – you can't have me! Do you think that you can just take whatever or whoever you want whenever you want? Do you know what it feels like to be cheated on, to be humiliated, to be replaced? I do! And Aydan doesn't deserve that! I'm not available to you!'

He looks at me for a long time as I stare back at him, trembling, desperately trying to somehow convey the integrity of my words despite not being sure that I really do mean them. I want to believe them, I want to believe I'm a decent person who doesn't hurt others deliberately, the way that I was hurt, before. He steps forward, forcing me back up against the wall as he stands before me, his serious expression questioning my outburst. He doesn't touch me again, but I can feel the warmth of him, and I know I'm already teetering on the edge of giving in despite my impassioned outburst.

'Aren't you, Paige? Aren't you available to me?' he asks softly.

'No,' I whisper unconvincingly, eyes filling again, hating myself and my desire for this man in equal measures. 'This needs to stop right now and I think it's best if you leave the writing group too. You're making it impossible for me!'

'If that's what you want, that's what I'll do,' he says. 'But is that what you really want?' He moves his hand slowly towards my face again and strokes my cheek gently. I close my eyes and rest my face against his palm, drowning in despair.

He knows I don't mean it. He knows he's got me.

Hours later, after he's left my bed and my house, I wake up alone in the dark, startled, dreaming of masked figures in gold Vectras spying on me, watching from the shadows wherever I go. Hardy stirs on the end of the bed and pads towards me before flopping down again. I reach out and stroke his soft, silky fur, grateful for his permanent companionship. As my heart begins to beat its normal pace again, what James and I did comes back to me in fragments, like a smashed mirror reflecting my weak will, my shameful deceit, my absolute pleasure at finally succumbing to him. I can barely believe it happened and I'm ashamed and euphoric in equal measure. Every single second was as sensational as I had fantasised about these past weeks, and I can still feel his touch imprinted on me.

My phone vibrates and I hope it's an email or a message from him – the first he will have ever sent. We haven't officially exchanged numbers yet but surely he's checked the group's contact details list by now?

Instead, the text is from the same unknown number from a few weeks ago and it contains only a link.

My addled, guilty brain struggles to comprehend its meaning, wondering if it's just spam, but I suspect it's not. I stare at it, half expecting to see an accusation from Aydan or, perhaps, inexplicably, a cruel meme behind its blue underlined text, acknowledging my unfaithfulness and the irony of it. With shaking hands, I click on the link and there, online, is a book. I stare at it. It's a book on Amazon with the same title as my manuscript – *Descent into Deceit* – yet it's not my name on the cover. A terrible suffocating feeling starts to shift its way up from my uneasy stomach, growing in strength as it fills my chest, my throat As I click the 'look inside' option with a racing heart, my worst fears are confirmed. I see that the first few pages are my pages – my words, my story, my secrets. It seems an author named K.M. Hardy has stolen them from me.

Chapter Twenty-Four

I struggle to breathe, to think straight. This can't be possible but I'm looking right at it. Aren't I? Am I dreaming? Is someone playing a trick on me? There are already a few reviews and they've all given four or five stars. I've written a book worthy of five-star reviews! But I haven't, have I? Because that's not my name on the cover. And all the "character" names inside have been changed. But I haven't uploaded it. I haven't published it. How has this happened?

I quickly click back onto the 'look inside' option – I distinctly recall amending a phrase on page two on my hard copy, so I check if it's been changed on this digital version. It has. Okay, so this is definitely the updated, second version of my manuscript, the one I started editing again after Hardy considered the first a tasty snack. Could someone have typed up the whole thing since the book fair a week and a half ago? Yes, it's possible, but would they have? I try to think back to when I last backed up my digital copy onto my memory stick, but I can't remember. Everything's been so scatty lately, including me. Did I put the memory stick somewhere safe, or could Hardy have chewed that too?

I slip my dressing gown over my naked body and rush downstairs, flipping on the hallway and living-room lights as I race to my desk and yank open each drawer in turn, rummaging around for the dog-shaped USB. It's not there in any of them. I check behind my computer, under the desk, feeling around the edges of the skirting board and along the windowsill. I even check in the half-dead plant pots but it's still nowhere to be seen.

'Think, Paige!' I command myself.

I sit down at my desk and do what I always do when I need to harness my thoughts: I grab a Post-it and pen and make a list. Who has been in my house in the past few weeks? Aydan, James, Sylvie, Renee, Joy, Lloyd and Kenny. Who was at the book fair? James, Sylvie, Renee, Joy, Lloyd, Kenny and Alexander? They're practically the same list! Who would want to steal my book? Sylvie, Renee, Joy, Lloyd, Kenny, James? Who would want to hurt me like this? I don't know!

Suddenly a light switches on in my brain, starkly illuminating another possibility, and I think I know who it must be.

The thought is enough to make me dart to the front window and sneak a look through the curtains. Hardy follows me inquisitively, no doubt perplexed about this late-night game, but up for it, nonetheless. I tentatively peer outside into the blackness, goose bumps puckering my skin, checking up and down the street for the Vectra, for a shadowy figure, for anything even remotely resembling the stature so familiar yet so alien to me now, but everything is silent and still. I sag to the floor, enveloping Hardy in my arms like a furry security blanket. He nuzzles into my neck and I'm grateful for the one thing in the world I can trust.

Morning arrives and Hardy's internal alarm clock has him nudging me to be let out into the backyard. I'm surprised for a split second to find myself on the floor leaning against the sofa but then, with a tidal wave of anxiety, I remember. I jerk up, my sore rib aching and my neck screaming in agony after being lodged at a weird angle while I slept. I scrabble around for my phone but it's still upstairs. I quickly unlock the back door for Hardy and run up to my bedroom. My still messy bed smells of James and sex, but I can't think about that now. Locating my phone, I check the message and the link again. I'm almost as shocked as I felt last night to see it's still there. My plagiarised book is still for sale on Amazon.

As I frown at it, brain in overdrive, another message comes through at the top of the screen. I'm relieved then horrified to see it's from Aydan.

> Good morning, AC. How are you today? I've got some great news – a whole four-day weekend off!!! How do you fancy a little break away to make up for all the overtime I've been working lately? Please say yes. A xxx

How can I possibly say yes after what I did with James last night? I must confess and bear Aydan's wrath or disappointment or upset, whatever his reaction may be. I have never seen him express any emotional extreme, nor him me come to think of it, which goes to show not only how shallowly we know each other, but also how little chance I've given our relationship. I've become the kind of person I detest.

It's still early so he won't be expecting a reply straight away, which buys me some time. I need to do some research into plagiarism first – I foresee myself typing *what to do when your manuscript is stolen* into Google.

I give Hardy his breakfast while I wait for the kettle to boil.

Then, once I've had a fortifying few sips of strong tea, I sit down at my desk to investigate further.

A few hours later I feel like I've read the whole of the internet on plagiarism. There's lots of helpful advice such as:

1. Track down plagiarists: you can use a plagiarism finding program to see if your work has been stolen.

2. Get legal representation but be sure to hire one that specialises in copyright infringement.

3. If your book is being sold without your permission it is fraud. Chances are good that if they're doing it to you, they're doing it to other authors as well.

It seems the best course of action is to go through the legal channels, except I can't afford to. Every penny I inherited from my grandpa went into buying my house and giving me a tiny bit of a buffer while I got back on my feet, either by growing my proofreading business, getting a publishing deal, or, if those plans fail miserably, getting a "proper" job. The latter still seems wildly impossible given my anxiety issues and just the thought of it is enough to make me as dizzy and nauseous as seeing my stolen book for sale made me. It seems, therefore, that I have no choice. I must find out who K.M. Hardy really is and confront them.

My phone vibrates again, and I realise I've forgotten to text Aydan back. I pick it up and see that I have a new email:

I thought it was about time we interacted electronically after connecting in a different way last night. Thank you for becoming available

<pre>
to me; you were most certainly worth the
wait. James xx
</pre>

My whole body flushes with the recollection of our 'connection' as I smile at the message, but as I'm absorbing it and reliving the delicious memory of James's mouth and hands and body on mine whilst actively fencing off my guilt, another text from Aydan flashes up on the screen, as though he knows my thoughts:

> Don't leave me hanging here, Paige! ;-) How does a weekend in the Lakes sound? A xxx

I've got a decision to make.

Chapter Twenty-Five

As I'm waiting to be collected, I reflect on my decision again. I waited as long as I dared before replying to Aydan, reverting to my usual method of decision-making and creating a pros and cons list. In the end I went with my head, not that either of them has my heart as such yet, but if I had chosen James without knowing who or what Sofia is to him, it would have made the situation even more complicated. Although now that James and I have slept together, all I can do is either lay myself at Aydan's mercy and hope he'll forgive me or choose to conceal my infidelity and hope he never finds out. I don't know which option I'm going to take yet. This long weekend in the Lake District will either make us or break us.

Speaking of breaking, telling James our night together was a mistake and that I've chosen to stay with Aydan was more difficult than I expected. For a writer, the words didn't come easily. Although we haven't "broken up" as we were never together, I still feel the loss of what we could have had keenly. However, I've come too far to throw away the beginnings of a stable relationship with Aydan in favour of an unpredictable man with an undefined status, whatever our connection. James didn't reply to my return email and perversely I want to make sure he's okay, but that would mean further involvement and I know that's not wise for my resolve. Instead, I clip Hardy's lead to his harness as I spot Aydan's car pulling up on the street outside.

On the journey to the Lake District, with Hardy happily ensconced in the back seat with my overnight bag, I morosely recount the story of seeing my book online to Aydan, obviously leaving out my antics preceding it. I become emotional as I describe the nausea I felt when I discovered my ideas, my hard work, were finally published yet attributed to someone else – this K.M. Hardy pirate.

Aydan is incredulous, as I knew he would be. 'That's insane, Paige! Why didn't you ring or text me straight away? I could have been there for you.'

'I was in shock, I think,' I reply. 'And I wanted to do a bit of investigating myself first, to see whether I could find out who they are and what I can do about it.'

'Well, who are they? What can you do about it? Surely it's illegal? Absolute fuckers!' He hits the top of the steering wheel with his palm to punctuate his opinion of my book thieves. Interesting that he assumes it's more than one person – could it be?

I sigh. His anger has reignited my frustration. 'Unfortunately, it's not as black and white as that. It's morally wrong, obviously, but apparently it happens quite often. I need to prove it's my intellectual property but I'm not sure how.'

'You must have draft copies at home? On a memory stick or on your computer?' Aydan glances at me quickly, placing a supportive hand on my knee and squeezing it whilst he drives. I'm reminded of James's hand on my knee in the cocktail bar and quickly block the memory.

'I do, well, I did. I saved my complete first draft on a

memory stick but that's gone missing, and my almost fully edited version was the hard copy that was stolen at the book fair,' I explain. Hearing myself say these words reminds me again how utterly stupid I've been with regards to not backing up or being careful enough with my precious book and I feel hopelessness override frustration once more.

Aydan squeezes my knee again in sympathy before moving his hand back to the steering wheel. 'Do you have your suspicions about who this K.M. Hardy bloke might be?' he asks.

I nod but don't voice my thoughts or comment on the fact he's made another assumption.

'Alexander, right, the son of the woman in your writing group? I said it was him! Little shit!' Aydan swears.

'I just don't think it is him,' I say quietly.

'But you said yourself he's a complete psycho.'

'I didn't say he was a psycho,' I reply with a frown, suddenly agitated by Aydan's theory that the thief must be Alexander and it's as simple as that. 'I said he's behaved strangely a couple of times and made me feel uncomfortable.'

'Yes – psychotic! And didn't he bad-mouth his own mum? I would never talk about my mum like that!'

I didn't realise Aydan was so passionately judgemental. Our weekend away is already enlightening me about this man I have chosen to stay with, and I realise that this is only the second time he has ever mentioned his mum. He glances at me again.

'If you don't think it's Alexander, which of the other writing group members do you think it is then?'

'I'm not sure it's any of them,' I say, watching the motorway ahead of us. 'I don't think any of them have a strong enough motive to steal my book.'

'What about hoity-toity-ideas-above-her-station Sylvie, or critical Lloyd who slags off the others? You said he's dropped you from proofreading his book now too. Aren't they in the frame? What about quiet Kenny – it's often the ones you'd never consider who are the real criminal masterminds!' He laughs, possibly attempting to lighten the mood.

I'm impressed he's remembered so much of what I've told him about my fellow writing group members and their foibles, even as I tut and playfully tap his hand for making fun of them. They are his descriptions, not mine, but he's clearly been a considerate listener. My heart softens towards him again; I've not given him enough credit for all his support. Yes, we haven't spent much time together, but the time we have had seems to have been filled with me talking about myself, and him absorbing what I've told him. That's such a fantastic quality in a boyfriend, and certainly not something I have experienced before, especially in the recent past.

I make the conscious decision to keep my mouth shut about James and my indiscretion. I have a man, right here, who is investing all this time in trying to understand my problem, wanting to help me, versus, for want of a better description, a one-night stand who has seen something he wants and taken it. I'm classing this weekend as a clean slate, washing away my sins in the Lakes, so to speak, and starting again, the very epitome of a perfect girlfriend.

'Anyway, let's change the subject,' I suggest. 'You're always indulging me and my dramas, even from afar when you're working. Tell me all about what's been going on with you lately.'

We enjoy a pit stop just after the halfway point of our journey for Hardy to stretch his fluffy little legs and drink some water, and for us to have something to eat. Aydan's been describing the 'office politics' going on at work and I'm beginning to get a better sense of the pressure he's under and why being on call is so necessary sometimes. I listened attentively, content in the knowledge that I've definitely made the right choice by staying with him before treating us to overpriced sandwiches and coffees. It's a small price to pay to say thank you for putting up with me.

A few hours later, after another quick stop for Aydan to make a work call, we pull up to The Burnside, a pet-friendly bed and breakfast in Keswick, and I gaze up at the olive-green façade in the beautiful tree-lined street overlooking the peaceful patchwork of countryside. The swinging sign outside the huge bay window announces *vacancies* and a colourful cascade of potted plants adorns each wide stone step leading up to the large front door.

'It's lovely,' I say, smiling as I turn towards Aydan. His expression, confusingly, doesn't match mine. In fact, he seems completely closed down. He opens his door and gets out of the car as Hardy begins to spin around, realising we are at our destination, and that he can finally escape the confines of the back seat. I look back at the guest house and see a man exit the porch doorway and begin to descend the stone steps. He's wearing a cap and a black leather jacket, blending in with the now overcast skies. Something about him looks familiar. I turn around to unclip Hardy's harness and as I do I see a gold Vectra parked a little way behind us on the opposite side of the road. My stomach lurches and I can instantly feel the pricklings of a panic attack. When I turn back, the leather-jacketed man is bent down next to my window, staring in. I scream out in shock.

He grins, opens my door and motions for me to get out.

I simply stare at him, this nightmarish apparition before my eyes. It's so strange how someone you once found so attractive can transform into the ugliest human you've ever met. Hardy's going mad in the back of the car, desperate to get out to greet him, this person he recognises. It's not his fault; dogs don't always realise that evil sometimes appears in a familiar form. A muscle memory kicks in, and I do as the man instructs. I'm a compliant coward once more.

'Hello, Paige,' he says with venom in his voice as I stand before him on shaky legs.

I look in dumb horror from him to Aydan – how am I going to explain this? Why is he here? Is this a coincidence or is he here for me? Why doesn't Aydan say something, anything?

'Shane?' I whisper the name I had hoped to erase from my vocabulary forever.

In the next split second, Aydan moves towards him, and I prepare myself for the confrontation. Aydan doesn't know who he is, but he must be able to sense the rabid animosity between this stranger and me, his girlfriend.

Yet to my absolute disbelief, Aydan takes Shane's hand, and they stand, fingers intertwined, united. The realisation is a sucker punch to my stomach: not only do they know each other but they're together.

A Dawn Raid

She always thought the phrase "a dawn raid" sounded quite poetic, yet it was anything but. The sun was still rising as the dog barked and barked, and the pounding on the front door intensified. The pounders definitely meant business, demanding entry, demanding access to their home, their lives. They sprinted downstairs, terrified, in dressing gowns and bare feet, clothing they wouldn't want anyone except their nearest and dearest to ever see them in, to be met with a team of police, efficient and authoritative.

'We have a warrant to search this property...' She stared uncomprehendingly at the piece of paper, clutching at the dog's collar to keep him at bay.

Just another day at the office for them but for her it was absolute destruction. It caused the hairline fracture in their already fragile relationship to deepen, to widen, to cause a crack big enough for the remaining fragments of love and trust she had left to plummet down and splinter at the bottom of the chasm. Her worst fears really had come true; there was no denying them now.

Of course he blustered, oscillating between acting

affronted and wounded, but she saw right through his act, finally. A kind female police detective led her away to the living room to question her. She was terrified she was culpable by association, despite being completely in the dark. She truly believed her innocence and naivety were her saving grace. No one could act that dumb successfully, surely. It was obvious she didn't know. With claw-like wizened fingers she held tight to the shameful knowledge that she had suspected but had been terrified of admitting her suspicions to anyone, not that there was really anyone to tell, not anymore.

Hours later, he eventually returned from being questioned by the police and instead of the meek and mild man she had expected, she watched the incandescent version of him raging against the invasion of the privacy he held so dear, of the injustice he had suffered, now that they were alone again. Only a few wires remained where his computers had been, thin black snakes either jutting upwards as though still attached umbilically or coiled on the floor in defeat.

'Fuckers!!!' he screamed, fists clenched, body bent in physical fury.

She was still crying, knowing that he hated her crying, but unable to stem the shocked tears. She was desperate to ask why the police had invaded their home out of the blue, why they had "seized" – their word – his computers and marched out of the house swiftly, transporting them like children being saved from a burning building, why they had questioned her about his character, his behaviour. Instead, she just wept.

He crouched down next to her and the dog on the floor. She thought for a moment he was going to reach out and comfort her, explain it was all a terrible mistake. She could smell his rancid morning breath, see the crusty sleep in the corner of his eye and a few dark nose hairs protruding from his nostrils. She felt disgusted by the face she once adored. Deception comes in many forms, and it's even more destructive when delivered by a familiar hand.

In one smooth move he twisted his fingers into her hair and roughly yanked her head back. 'Tell anyone about this and you'll regret it.'

— *Descent into Deceit*

Chapter Twenty-Six

I feel like I've been punctured, pierced with a sharp object, and no breath remains within me. I'm winded, deflated, light-headed. I simply stare at them, paralysed with shock.

'Here's what's going to happen, Paige,' Shane begins. 'You and Aydan are going to check into the guest house and wait for me. You'll give Aydan your phone so you can't do anything silly like ring someone, although, if memory serves, I doubt there'll be anyone to call anyway. I'll be back soon. Then we'll have a proper catch-up.' He kisses Aydan on the mouth, and I nearly retch at the thought of Aydan kissing me only hours before. He walks assuredly to his gold Vectra, his pride and joy, gets in without looking back and drives away. What a fool I've been.

Aydan hands me my overnight bag, takes Hardy's lead from me and like a pre-programmed robot, unable to think for myself, I follow him up the steps towards the guest-house door.

After holding his hand out for my phone, which I obediently give him, Aydan checks us in. The middle-aged lady on reception doesn't have a clue that I'm there under duress as she's too busy fussing Hardy to notice my frozen body language.

Aydan thanks her for the room key she passes to him then guides me upstairs, a firm hand on my back. We must look to all intents and purposes like an ordinary couple here for a weekend away – exactly what I thought we were just half an hour ago. My mind is splintering, the jagged edges scratching awkwardly against each other, unable to make sense of this new reality I find myself in. Aydan and Shane? No, it can't be true, can it?

Once in the room, which I miserably register is lovely, Aydan motions for me to sit down on the bed and takes one of the plump pastel armchairs in the bay window for himself. He hasn't spoken to me since we were in the car and has now shed the version I knew of him like a snake's skin. It's such a strange feeling to suddenly feel scared of someone you thought you knew, and although it's the second time it's happened to me, I still don't know how to handle it any better now than then. Hardy lies on the floor by my feet, part of our artificial tableau of happiness in this pretty room.

'Aydan, please talk to me,' I attempt, still struggling to comprehend this hideous parallel universe. 'How do you know Shane? Why is he here?'

He refuses to even look at me, instead concentrating on something on his phone, my pleas for information falling on deaf ears. This man is now a stranger.

After half an hour of excruciating silence later, Shane returns and sidles into the room as though he owns it and sits proprietorially on the arm of Aydan's chair, legs wide, confident. Aydan immediately puts his phone away, alert now, as though a puppeteer has suddenly brought him to life on stage. He obviously told Shane exactly where we were and there's absolutely no doubt in my mind that Shane charmed the receptionist to let him up, such is the power he wields with people who don't know the rotten core underneath the handsome mask. Trusting traitor Hardy, recognising Shane again, attempts to fondly greet this long-lost acquaintance he spent the first few months of his life around. Shane, knowing how much it will torture me to see my dog anywhere near him, responds to Hardy's tail wagging request and fusses him exaggeratedly. I click my fingers, desperately willing my furry boy to obey my command to return to my side.

'Hardy, come here!' My voice breaks as I point to the floor next to me. After a moment Hardy complies and Shane sniggers his amusement.

'How are you out of prison already?' I ask. It's the main question I need to know the answer to. He was sentenced to four years in December 2013 so he should be safely behind bars until the end of this year.

He flashes a grin at me, and I'm catapulted back to the first time we ever met, in that remote pub car park, when I held so much hope about him and us, before I knew what he really was.

'Early release for good behaviour,' he says cheerily. Good behaviour? What a joke. But the new shadows under his eyes tell a different tale: it's been hard for him inside. I'm glad.

'How did you find me?' I fire at him next. I thought I'd moved far enough away from the scandal of our past life together to not be found easily, especially by a fucked up, locked up ex-fiancé. I thought I'd been careful.

'You really are that stupid, aren't you?' he sneers. 'Thanks to my trusted network I've been able to keep tabs on you for a long time, since you used to follow *me* to try to catch me out. But you never actually caught me out, did you? For anything, despite your best efforts.'

I'm shaking, struggling to comprehend my own naivety, painfully remembering all the agonising time I lost watching for him from my car, waiting for proof that he was cheating on me, sending myself half insane with only my overactive imagination for company. Yet everything I suspected I was right about. Unfortunately, no comfort came with the belated confirmation.

'Do you know what it's like, seeing your face plastered across the local news rags, banged to rights, without any hard evidence?' he asks, his mouth twisted into a sneer.

'A team of police swarming inside the house and seizing your computers was evidence!' I cry. 'And your subsequent conviction and jail time following yet more evidence proved I was right!'

He shakes his head. 'No. Your "anonymous" tip-off to your journalist friend made me a pariah in the community. You caused that. I couldn't get a job and the house was spray-painted with vile although unimaginative, words. And that led to some extremely offensive and disturbing trolling and threats.'

I'm aghast at his audacity, appalled by his mental machinations, his obstinate refusal to take ownership of his crimes, and I can't stop myself from shouting out, my carefully constructed dam breaking, years of pent-up rage escaping. 'What? That's the bit you're focusing on? You're utterly delusional! And you didn't even want a job; you were happy to claim permanent sick-note status and live off your mum and stepdad's handouts in your free house! A grown man, a liar of the worst kind, and still subsidised by his mummy!' I reach down to soothe Hardy who's absorbing my distress and starting to squeak.

He points a finger towards me, his face a gnarled mask of malice. 'A free house that I was forced to move out of, because of you. Bitch'

Hardy ruffs gently as there's a knock on the door and relief washes through me – the receptionist must have heard my shouts. She'll be able to help me.

Aydan, who has been watching our exchange with a stony expression, stands and crosses the room, pausing before depressing the handle. He glances back at Shane, who is sucking his teeth, his nostrils flaring, before finally speaking to me.

'Paige, I'd like to introduce you to my mum.' Aydan smirks. He opens the door and standing there on the threshold is Joy.

Chapter Twenty-Seven

If I thought I was surprised to see Shane, nothing could have prepared me for the shock of seeing Joy in the doorway. I feel physically assaulted; the pain is so intense.

Joy greets her son warmly before crossing over to Shane and embracing him in a heartfelt hug too. He dwarfs her and she looks fragile in his strong arms, although I know she's anything but.

'What... what's going on?' I manage to whisper.

The look she gives me could sour milk. It's as though another person entirely is inhabiting Joy's body, her mannerisms, expressions and image all wrong. Gone is the red lipstick, the back-combed helmet hair, the patterned clothes. She's an 'after' on a makeover – or rather, makeunder – show.

'I've known Shane since he was a little boy,' she begins, her voice almost unrecognisable in its new tone and timbre, devoid of her previous affectations. 'Back when I was married, my husband and I lived down the road from Shane's mum – she was a single mother struggling to cope and I helped out with babysitting, and the like. Shane spent more time at our house than he did at his own. Unfortunately, Shane's mother saw the twinkle in my husband's eye and off they went, together, leaving my boy without a father and me with another surrogate son, which is what I considered Shane to be, from the outset. As you can imagine, I was distraught, but I soldiered on, as you do, and I single-handedly raised a wonderful young man, my Aydan.' She strokes Aydan's cheek affectionately. 'But my son had his fair share of troubles, despite my best efforts. He struggled mentally, he struggled with his sexuality, he struggled to really understand himself, all afflictions no doubt either caused or exacerbated by the absence of his father.'

I'm agog as she speaks. All her old, unique Joy-ness has gone, replaced with a no-nonsense, ordinary demeanour. I realise it was all an act, a three-dimensional character she created – the scattiness, the exuberance, the friendliness. I feel myself sag under the disappointment of what a terribly naive judge of character I am; nobody can really be trusted, it seems.

'And then in 2013,' she continues, 'he found himself again when he and his best friend were reunited. Shane was forced to leave his home to escape the shame you brought on him, and the accusations you levied against him when you left him. Thank God he tracked us down when he did.'

'He brought it all on himself,' I reiterate, pressing my lips together stubbornly, daring to look her in her non false-lashed eye.

'No!' She rounds on me, propelling the word out with force. 'The sweet little boy I knew all those years ago, and the man before me today is simply not capable of the things you accused him of! The things you made the police believe!'

'I didn't accuse him. I told the truth, and the police investigated. People had a right to know there was a paedophile living in their midst!'

Joy slaps me hard across the face and I recoil from the sting as Hardy stands and lets out a warning bark. She did once say she can hold a grudge like a cursed gypsy, and she's certainly proving that now.

'Don't you dare utter that word!' she spits, as though expelling any residue of it from her own mouth. 'When I saw him again after all those years, he was a broken man seeking refuge from a baying mob!' She reaches for Shane's hand and clutches it. 'We rebuilt him, Aydan and I. Regular prison visits. Requesting appeal after appeal. As a consequence, Aydan and Shane fell in love. I gave them my full blessing; it was as though life had come full circle.'

I want to snigger a scathing retort but my burning cheek beneath my palm reminds me I would be better off keeping quiet.

'So you messed with my head and stole my manuscript,' I state, the pieces falling into place.

'Oh, it was easy to manipulate you and watch you crumble, Paige, you're not exactly made of strong stuff.' She chuckles nastily. 'I created a fun persona and joined the same writing group Aydan found out you had joined, intending to befriend then unnerve you, whispering rumours about your professionalism to the others for starters, then progress to making your life a living hell, as you made Shane's. But then you announced you had written your book! From the sneaky peeks I made sure I took, and the little snippets I teased out of you, I soon knew it was about you and Shane!? You were so smug, so proud of yourself and your achievement, but I realised that not only stealing it but publishing it online and actually making money from it could be the perfect payback both emotionally and financially for poor Shane. He is the main character, after all, and therefore perfectly entitled to a share of the royalties.'

I listen to her proud confession – Joy successfully manipulated the other writing group members' opinions of me for months. That perhaps explains why Lloyd did a swift about turn on me proofreading his manuscript, which unbalanced my confidence and lost me my only paying client. I thought his opinion of me had changed due to the book fair manuscript theft, but of course, she must have orchestrated that as well! Did the others believe her lies too? Is that why my mental health was so freely commented on?

I look around at the three faces before me, each looking back, full of scorn and hatred. 'And what about you?' I ask Aydan, tears threatening to fall. 'Did you ever want to be an author or was our first meeting a set-up? Was any of it true – your book, your dyslexia, your house, your work? What was I to you?'

'Don't you mean what was he to you?' Shane replies for him. 'He was the original plan A – his objective was to get close to you then ruin you, just like you ruined me. But then Joy suggested a more furtive quest – gleefully, may I add – and we had a two-pronged attack. This way we could decimate your personal and professional life at the same time.' He snaps his fingers to reinforce his point.

'You bastard,' I say, my voice quivering with emotion. The thought of them all in a prison visiting room discussing my downfall and constructing such an elaborate plan to "get back" at me when Shane is the villain here both sickens and saddens me.

'Well, as I don't know my father, I am indeed a bastard,' he says chirpily. 'My mum was Aydan's dad's fancy piece for a while, but he moved on a long time ago, and so did my mum. She's now living the high life abroad with another sugar daddy and this one isn't as keen to help me out with money, which is why your book is going to go some way to subsidising our new life. Joy is like a mother to me, in the absence of my own selfish excuse for one, and I want to repay her for her kindness, care and bel ef in me. We've all been screwed over by those closest to us.'

I seethe; numb with fury.

'Oh, it's doing quite well, by the way – your book,' he continues. 'Aydan is quite the IT genius and marketing whizz, and he's doing an amazing job promoting it online with promos and paid ads And Joy came up with the genius idea of doing all this again and again – there are writing groups all over the place, all containing naïve little trusting writers, just like you. Easy to befriend and easy to hoodwink. Screwing over strangers won't give us as much satisfaction as screwing you over already has, Paige, but it's got the potential to be a good little earner judging by the sales of your book. You should be proud of yourself, Agatha Christie!' he says, using Aydan's affectionate refrain for me. My blood boils.

'You're the worst kind–'

'Sticks and stones,' he interrupts. 'Because your words will certainly not hurt me, not now they're making us money.' He gives me a self-satisfied smirk and I swallow down my disgust.

'Aydan?' I try again to appeal to the better nature I still believe he has, somewhere. Shane is running this show, not him. 'Why are you doing this?' I ask.

'Why am I doing what?' He shrugs casually but his expression is severe. 'Backing up the man I love against the worst thing anybody can be accused of? A man I've known for over twenty years versus your pathetic claims? He's not capable of that! And no, none of it was true, not my working in Scotland, not my dyslexia, not even writing a book... why would I bother with that when we can pass others off as our own? It was all a carefully constructed cover story as soon as we'd tracked you down, which wasn't difficult, by the way. None of it was – finding your phone number, making you believe I fancied you, fucking you hard like the little slut you are. Nice little perk of the job, if you ask me; Shane taught you well. And you believed it all, you pathetic bitch!'

His face is twisted with disdain, a doppelganger to the Aydan I met only a few weeks ago. I feel as though I'm going to be sick. 'It was particularly entertaining winding you up about who could have stolen your manuscript when the real culprit – Mum – was right under your nose,' he adds. Shane chuckles and nods, his dark eyes glinting with pleasure.

'How dare you question him anyway, you little tramp!' intercepts Joy. 'When you've been seeing another man behind his back and simpering about being caught between the two of them. It's you who needs help for your excessive sexual impulses!' sneers Joy.

I ignore her and her double standard statements. The woman is scarily, wilfully ignorant to Shane's sexual depravity and the fact that her own son seduced me at his boyfriend's command. But the mention of James sparks another question. I'm desperate for answers, desperate to understand how Aydan has been able to play such a convincing role from the beginning.

'Aydan, did you really meet James at a property conference?' I ask.

He huffs out a delighted laugh. 'Yes, that bit was true, actually. Weird coincidence running into him, but it reinforced my cover from the off. Property is something I'm interested in, but we need some more capital to increase our rental portfolio; one tiny house in Hull and one in Leeds won't give us the lavish lifestyle we're after. It's difficult for Shane to get a proper job now, thanks to his unjust criminal record as well as a simple Google search alerting any possible employer to the revenge article you commissioned.' He makes air quotes around the word "proper" before jabbing his finger in my direction. 'So we need more ways of making money – that's where your book comes in, as well as all the others we're going to add to our portfolio.'

'A revenge article?' I shout. 'I told the truth!' But my protest falls on deaf ears yet again.

Shane rolls his eyes as if I'm nothing more than a child lying about breaking a toy. 'We're leaving now, Paige,' he informs me, gesturing to his entourage as he closes in. He leans down to stroke Hardy again and my boy sits up, welcoming the attention whilst keeping one eye on me. He must sense my intense unease. 'But here's what you're going to do, or rather not do...' he continues watching Hardy watching me. 'You're not going to do anything at all. We're going to continue making money from your book and if you intervene in any way, we'll not only continue to ruin your professional reputation and then what remains of your sorry little life, but poor Hardy here will also suffer.' He clamps his left hand hard around Hardy's snout as he finally locks up at me. My beloved dog, realising this man suddenly represents danger, tries to pull backwards out of Shane's grasp but is unable to free himself from the strong grip and begins to whimper.

'Stop!' I cry, lunging forwards. 'Leave him alone!'

Shane pushes me back with his other hand, preventing me from reaching Hardy, now clearly in distress. I'm suddenly fearfully wondering whether he ever hurt puppy Hardy in the past, when they were alone in the house while I was always out at work, earning extra money to top up Shane's already considerable handouts that still never seemed to cover the bills. I cry out again at the retrospective realisation of all of it.

'Are we clear?' Shane asks, eyes mocking, full of power and control.

'Yes!' I say, willing to agree to anything to prevent Hardy being seriously harmed.

'Say it – say you'll do absolutely nothing.'

'I won't do anything at all, just please let him go!' I'm in tears, clawing at Shane's arm, unable to cope with seeing Hardy's discomfort and desperation to wrench himself free. I want to shout at Joy and Aydan, 'Look! See what kind of man he really is – he preys on children *and* animals!' but they simply watch benignly, like brainwashed cult members.

He releases Hardy like a spring, and Hardy paws twice at his snout before scuttling under my legs to safety, trembling.

'Good girl. You're nothing but a blank Paige now.' Shane laughs, amused at his own cutting pun.

'Toodle-pip, darling!' Joy cruelly affects her alter ego one last time as all three of these strangers finally leave me alone again, abandoned at the bed and breakfast.

Hardy nuzzles against me, still offering comfort despite his own ordeal and I scoot down next to him on the floor, soothing him with strokes and words of reassurance as my tears splash unchecked onto his fur.

Chapter Twenty-Eight

I sit soothing Hardy – and myself – for a long time. He seems to understand my anguish in that way that dogs do and just rests his head on my lap while I cry out the shock and devastation of the situation. It was bad enough seeing Shane again after all these months but to have been double-crossed by Aydan and Joy too is almost too much for me to bear and feels like an even worse betrayal than Shane's original lies and deceit. Is everyone in my life destined to feed me nothing but a twisted, fictitious version of themselves? Am I culpable somehow?

An image of my grandpa flashes into my mind – spittle flying from his mouth as he screamed at me, my hands raised as I cowered from his frequent slaps, the smell of alcohol on his sour breath. A terrifying giant of a man riddled with secrets and untruths that I didn't discover until after his death, after teenage years interwoven with confusion and grief. He was driving on the night of the accident, my parents his passengers when they were killed. He was over the limit yet under the threshold for jail time so got away with a suspended sentence and a few minor injuries, as well as a sullen, traumatised twelve-year-old me, in the absence of anyone else in line for the responsibility.

He definitely didn't want me though. He made that quite clear. His demise nearly a year and a half ago – liver failure – created the catapult I used to launch my new life. The sale of his home, minus settling his debts, formed my inheritance. He'd already liquified – literally – what my parents had left me. But did I invite his hatred; make things more difficult for him? I must have done. No wonder he treated me like he did; I was a liability, a restriction, a doormat. Just like I was with Shane.

And now I've not only pushed James away, but I might have alienated my writing group thanks to Joy's insidious mutterings, and possibly jeopardised my business too. The three positives I had going for me, my reasons for carrying on, probably all gone.

I think back over all the wrong choices I have made and see a pattern emerging: poor, meek Paige, getting trampled on emotionally and physically, transitioning from job to job, man to man, and home to home with no clear purpose, no direction. Getting caught up with the wrong people, too trusting, too pliable, too flimsy for my own good. It needs to stop. I need to take action and claim the life I want instead of letting others dictate the terms. It's finally time to fight back.

A while later, after I have calmed my heaving sobs and cleaned my puffy, tear-stained face, I venture downstairs with renewed hope to ask the hotel receptionist if the hotel has a communal computer I could use to look for alternative accommodation seeing as Aydan took my phone. I know I can't stay here. I daren't risk walking Hardy to a nearby library, or internet café, if there are any in such a remote location, for fear of Shane, Aydan and Joy still being in the vicinity, as well as there potentially being a *no dogs allowed* rule. Not that I ever would, but now more than ever, I'm not prepared to leave Hardy outside alone anywhere, even for a matter of moments.

Logging on to the ancient guest house computer seems to take an age, cruelly reminding me of the intermittent internet connection I had – and often cursed – when Shane and I first met and talked online, preventing us from talking for hours as I would have welcomed back then. I tap my foot impatiently as the shame of being hoodwinked by him rears up again, threatening to lurch its way out of me. I swallow it down, knowing I won't be able to keep it at bay for long. Out of habit I log on to my emails first from the Google home page, and I'm both shocked and surprised to see a message from James!

```
Whatever it takes for you to trust me,
I'll do it. James xx
```

He saw through my half-hearted brush-off and is refusing to take no for an answer! My head is pounding with uncertainty – should I trust him?

Needing quick, first-hand information, I scurry back to reception to check where the dog-friendly B&Bs and pubs are in the next village before replying to his email. I decide to take a chance and reply with a location and a time, nothing more. If he's genuine and he really has feelings for me, I've got to believe in his commitment and trust that he'll come.

In the meantime, I need to think. I borrow the notepad and pen from beside the computer and sit in the guest lounge with Hardy by my chair, a water bowl within his reach. It's time for a list. I once read that when you don't know what to do, just do the next right thing, whatever that might mean. I consider my limited options for the immediate future:

— Check out of here
— Walk to next village when dark
— Check in somewhere new
— Meet James?

Beyond that, I don't really know what could or should happen. If James doesn't show up, I dread to think what that might do to the tiny shred of positivity I've got left.

As per my list, I check out of the bed and breakfast without staying the night. Of course, nobody else has paid for the room and it's too late to cancel the booking, so I offer up my debit card, dipping into my dwindling savings. I couldn't possibly sleep here; the room is contaminated with the presence of Shane, Aydan and Joy. Following the receptionist's recommendations, Hardy and I set off cautiously towards the next village as soon as dusk begins to blanket the already grey sky.

Despite the long walk, by the time I've checked us into our alternative lodgings for the night, there's still two hours to kill until the time I specified in my email to James, to give him enough time to drive here from Hull. But walking has given me plenty of time to overthink the situation – what if he didn't see the email straight away? What if he is with Sofia and he's been stringing me along? What if he simply decides I'm not worth the effort? I didn't exactly explain myself so he might be having second thoughts, annoyed that I'm making demands or sending him on a wild goose chase of some sort. Everything Shane made me believe about myself still affects my thought processes so savagely.

I feed Hardy, freshen up and get changed before making my way to the local pub. I settle into a cosy corner with a drink, in an armchair facing the door. My stomach rumbles but the thought of eating reminds me of the carefree lunch I shared with Aydan only hours before and swiftly steals my appetite. He really stayed in character right up until the bitter end. He and his mother both deserve an award for their professional performances.

It's raining heavily now, and the pitched pub roof feels as

though it's vibrating with the pressure of it, matching the panic pulsing through me as more and more time ticks by. As I'm about to give up and head back to the B&B, the sorrow weighing me down like a physical mass, a familiar figure finally enters the pub, pulling down his drenched hood as the door swings closed behind him. He looks around the bar, searching for me. Finally, we lock eyes. My heart swells with gratitude and relief. James Locksley is here.

Chapter Twenty-Nine

James returns from the bar with our drinks and I waste no time telling him everything, the words cascading out of me as the locked box lid opens. Trembling, I tell him about my abusive relationship with Shane and the shocking reason I left him, my supposed fresh start in Hull after the death of my horrible grandad, my false relationship with Aydan and my wolf in sheep's clothing friendship with Joy, and how they are all interlinked. I tell him about Joy's attempt at my character assassination and he confirms he's heard her slyly undermining my mental health at our writing group meetings. He tells me he categorically never believed any of her rumours and tried more than once to warn me what was going on, but I refused to speak to him. I'm devastated to have been so distrusting of him.

Finally, I tell him about my novel and its new author – K.M. Hardy. While I had been waiting for him to arrive, I think I figured out their cruel Frankenstein pen name: K for Aydan and Shane's surnames (Keyes and Kennedy respectively), M for McLellan, Joy's surname, and a nod to me through Hardy's name. I've got to grudgingly admit, they really thought it through – as well as their threats towards Hardy, towards me. I feel squashed underfoot, suffocated by the inability to react, to seek retribution for this injustice.

James looks deep in thought. 'So, your book – it's autobiographical?'

'It's based on what happened with Shane, yes, but it's framed as a novel, not a memoir. Write what you know, so they say. Shane feels that as he was the inspiration for the book, he deserves the rewards, which is a paradox given that he continues to deny it all despite being convicted of attempting to groom young boys through an online game.'

'But he's not smart enough to comprehend the reason for you writing it in the first place?' asks James, looking at me sympathetically.

'That's just it, he clearly is really smart. He fooled me and manipulated me for two years, he's got Aydan and Joy wrapped around his little finger, and I've no doubt there are others too. He's a master of deceit.' I sigh and slump back in my seat, reaching down to pat Hardy.

'How do you think he's doing it all? If he's a sex offender, will he be allowed computers or access to the internet now he's out of prison?' James asks, taking a swig of his beer.

'I really don't know, but he'll have access to Aydan's anyway. Trust me this man can do virtually anything using a computer so I doubt not having his own will ever stop him. Apparently, Aydan's a tech whizz too,' I tell him, miserably.

James frowns. 'And there was me telling you I thought that Aydan seemed like a good bloke. I actually liked him when we met at the property auction in Leeds.'

'That was his nice guy act – practice makes perfect,' I say miserably

He taps a finger against the edge of the table as though he's had an idea. 'You know, Kenny and I were talking at the book fair. Despite his unassuming demeanour, he was quite the formidable detective inspector in his younger years. I bet he could put us in touch with the right person to find Shane.'

'Kenny was a detective?' I repeat, surprised. 'But he's so... shy!' I finally settle on.

James nods in agreement before revealing more. 'He had a bit of a breakdown after his wife was killed in a hit-and-run. Lost faith in the system after the driver got off with a fine. Took early retirement.'

'Poor Kenny. I had no idea,' I say, in awe of his ability to put on such a stoic front in the face of such tragedy as well as feeling slightly ashamed of always being so wrapped up in my own troubles to have ever bothered trying to find out more about him.

'Lloyd's got publishing contacts too and I bet he'll know someone who could help you prove the plagiarism,' adds James.

Despite imbuing me with a kernel of hope that I could challenge these circumstances, the memory of Shane's hand clamped around Hardy's snout reminds me otherwise. 'But what about the repercussions – they'll hurt Hardy and ruin me!'

'Paige.' His voice is soft and he gently takes my hand in his. 'They've lied to you, they've stolen from you, they've threatened you and they've admitted they're going to do it to others too. We've got to challenge them.'

'But how?' I ask pathetically, again seeing myself as the timid, defeated person Shane sculpted with his psychological torment. 'Even if Kenny and Lloyd do want to help me – and it's a big if with Lloyd considering he thinks I'm mentally unstable right now – Shane, Aydan and Joy have gone. Aydan lied to me about living in a rented house in Hull, Joy never held a writing group meeting at her house because of her supposed renovations – another lie, no doubt – and now I've found out she actually lives in Leeds somewhere with Aydan and Shane. Except I've no idea where and they've published my book under a pseudonym, not any of their own names. Even if I could find them it's still my word against theirs.' My own voice sounds hollow and hopeless.

'Whatever's gone on with you and Lloyd, I know he'll want to help once I tell him, and the others, what Joy's been up to with her rumours. We've got to try; your career and reputation – your new life – are at stake.'

I feel bolstered by his continued use of the word "we" – could we, as a team, really salvage something out of this mess? I've been used and tricked in the worst ways, making me wary of accepting help, yet I know that left to my own devices I may lose my nerve and retreat from the world and let them win, too much of a coward to fight.

A little while later, after we've finished our drinks and I'm all talked out, James walks me back to the nearby guest house. The rain has finally eased but the damp air and moist fog feel quite oppressive, making my already addled brain even more fuzzy with exhaustion. It's been quite the day, a far-fetched plot in a story not yet resolved. Hardy ambles slightly ahead of us, quickly sniffing the occasional lamp post and post box as we wend our way through the village, retracing my steps from earlier in reverse.

I try not to think about what will happen once we reach the guest house and just enjoy the feeling of James's hand in mine and the unusual weightlessness in my heart now I've offloaded my story, my secrets. I've been far too quick to trust in the past, resulting in terrible consequences, but that doesn't mean my judgement about everyone is wrong, that all my decisions are bad ones. I need to learn from the experience and move past it, properly. Either I trust James now, wholeheartedly, or I spend whatever time we have on whatever this is looking for signs of deceit, making myself miserable. That's not how I want to live my life.

We slow to a stop outside the guest house, and I open the latch on the tall wrought-iron gate. The entrance to the Victorian-style end of terrace is at the side of the house rather than the front and the narrow street we're standing on is gloomy but sheltered. We gaze at each other for a few moments in the shadows, both seemingly unaware of the correct protocol for this bizarre situation we've found ourselves in. I want him to lead me inside, to hold me while I sleep, to be there with me all night. I want to feel not alone for the first time in a long time. It's impossible for me to articulate this, yet somehow, he already knows. He pushes through the gate, turning back to offer me his hand, the soft light from the guest house porch falling gently on his kind, handsome face.

'Come on,' he says simply. So, I do.

Chapter Thirty

I wake early, Hardy lying heavily on my legs. As my brain stretches towards consciousness, I open my eyes to see floral curtains covering a deep bay window, which is generous considering the size of the small double room. I frown, momentarily disorientated, before the events of the previous day assault me with a ferocious slap, much like the one delivered by the unfamiliar version of Joy. I recall driving here with Aydan, being ambushed by Shane, then Joy, being threatened, being devastated, being helped... I look over to my right at James and smile despite everything; perhaps yesterday wasn't all bad.

I lie here, not moving, not wanting to break the spell but Hardy stirs, jumps off the bed and begins twirling at the door, his signal to be let out. I climb begrudgingly out of bed, pull on yesterday's clothes, clip on his harness and lead, and slip outside as quietly as I possibly can with my excitable border collie. Now that I'm awake my mind is whirring with the possibilities and responsibilities of the day, the week, the month ahead. I'm suddenly eager to get going, to reassemble myself, to feel how I used to feel before I met Shane.

The bed is empty when I return to the room after taking

Hardy on a lap of the wraparound garden, and my heart catches in my throat.

'James?' I say. Then louder, 'James?'

I immediately think the worst: he's realised what a liability I am, how complicated this situation is and decided to clear off, after all. A flash of fury also bubbles up with the memory of last night, of us lying together peacefully, James stroking my hair as I cried over my recollections of my abusive relationships as a meek granddaughter and fiancée, as well as my sorrowful realisation that Aydan, Shane or Joy had probably thrown away my favourite photo of my parents after Joy stole my bag from the book fair. That particularly stung. I finally let him in and he must have realised how difficult that was for me, yet he's clearly rejected me too.

'In here,' he shouts from the en suite and my insecurities of a moment before fade instantly into nothingness. The relief is immense. I push open the door and see the blurry outline of him in the small shower cubicle, steam rising and gravitating over the chequered tiled floor to the undressed sash window. He peeks out from behind the screen, water dripping down his face and his muscular shoulders. 'Fancy joining me?' he asks with a cheeky smile.

I giggle. 'We can't both fit in there!'

'Why don't we try?' he asks meaningfully, and I know he doesn't just mean the shower.

I laugh again, already peeling off my top.

An hour later, after our squashed but giggly shower and a freshly prepared hearty Sunday breakfast in the guest house's dining room, the three of us walk briskly to James's car which he left parked at the pub last night, worried about being over the limit to drive after the hours we spent drinking and talking. James is typing on his phone as quickly as we walk. I thought I would really miss mine, but it feels weirdly freeing not being able to use it.

'Okay, I've emailed Kenny and Lloyd and asked to meet with them both first thing tomorrow.' He looks at his watch. 'We should be back in Hull by early afternoon – I've suggested holding the meeting at my place. I need to collect Red later and then we can do a bit of our own research before speaking with them to find out what our options are.'

'Who has Red?' I ask, feeling a mix of pleasure at the way he organised things to come to my rescue, and guilt that I hadn't even remembered his responsibility for her. Perhaps a part of me assumed he would bring her.

'My next-door neighbour jumped at the chance to dog sit,' he responds as his phone rings. My heart clutches at the hope that it's either Kenny or Lloyd responding to James's meeting request but instead of answering the call he declines it. I'm momentarily pleased that his sole focus is on me until a few seconds later a text pings its arrival. He tuts and slows for a few seconds, opening the message then staring at it. When he looks back at me a strange expression crosses his face, an expression I don't know him well enough to decipher yet.

'What is it?' I ask, eventually, the silence prolonged.

'It's Sofia – my wife,' he says.

We begin driving, in silence save for Hardy's panting on the back seat. I open the window for him and he immediately pokes his snout through, sniffing the drizzling country air. His joyous reflection in the wing mirror would normally make me smile but I'm too anxious, hands clasped in my lap, pointlessly predicting and overthinking the contents of James's text and his unreadable reaction to it.

'Go on then, why didn't you tell me Sofia was your wife?' I ask, unable to bear the silence any longer.

'She claims she has cancer.' James chances a glance at me, no doubt gauging my reaction to one word in particular.

'Claims? What... you don't believe her?' I ask, shocked.

James runs a hand down his face and sighs heavily. 'I sound like a complete bastard, don't I?'

He misunderstands me. My shock isn't related to his scepticism of his wife's claim, it's shock at the parallels of our lives.

'No, that's not...' I shake my head; I can't believe the coincidence. 'Shane once lied about having cancer too.' James flicks an incredulous glance at me, and I nod. What a bizarre little club we're in. I sigh and turn to gaze out of the windscreen at the beautiful, unspoilt scenery surrounding us, the antonym to my internal chaos. 'It was fairly early on in our relationship when he was still working as a car salesman. He hadn't been to work for a few days but by then he'd begun to call in sick quite often, once he'd realised that work actually meant showing up and making an effort. Or perhaps people were already starting to see through him – people quicker on the uptake than me,' I say ruefully. 'Anyway, one day I was running late leaving myself, and his manager turned up to either check he was all right or check up on him. I was behind the side gate about to get into my car, and I heard every word of their conversation. The easy way he just said it: "I'm having some tests... it might be cancer". He was obviously convincing as the manager became instantly sympathetic. It was the first I'd ever heard of it and of course, nothing came of this supposed scare. He really was the lowest of the low.'

'Oh, Paige, I'm so sorry. Why didn't you leave him then?'
I look across at him and I'm relieved to see there's no

judgement in his expression; he's genuinely interested in my answer although I suspect he already understands.

'Why don't you leave her?' I counter, assuming they're still together if he's referring to Sofia as his wife in the present tense.

He frowns intensely. 'I don't know how to prove it – how can you accuse someone of making up a cancer diagnosis?'

'Why do you suspect she has?'

He sighs again. 'She was ill, a long time ago, when we were first married. Crohn's. She had surgery to remove part of her digestive system. Over the years she learnt how to manage it, but she would always joke about how much she loved being a patient, the care and attention that came with it. If ever we had a rough patch, she would always have a flare-up and, of course, I would do all that I could to help her, and our problems would be papered over. Then she had an affair with someone she met in her Crohn's Facebook group of all things!' He barks a laugh before becoming serious once more. 'She confessed straight away, begged for forgiveness, tried to justify it by saying he understood her in a way I couldn't. She considered it a terrible mistake, but the damage was done, and I left. Got my own place. That was when I wrote my book, actually, in the weeks following. It was a way to keep busy, to stop torturing myself with mental images of her being unfaithful. I was so angry and disappointed.'

I watch him as he's talking, the grief, the anguish, the guilt scored into his face. His knuckles are white mounds as he grips the steering wheel. This is hard for him to confess to – the suspicion of his own wife lying about something so serious, despite their history and clear evidence of her deceitful nature. I feel sad that we've both been unlucky enough to have been immersed in such manipulative relationships. He takes a ragged breath, caught up in his memories, and continues his story.

'A few months after I left, she got in touch saying she was

having tests for a tumour. We hadn't made any progress towards discussing a divorce – she flatly refused to whenever I brought it up – and I believed her when she told me she had been too sick with worry about her health. We tried again. I thought she was so strong, the way she coped with it, so dignified. She never wanted me to accompany her to any of her appointments, didn't want my life or work disrupted because of her. Of course, I supported her in other ways but then, magically, the tumour just disappeared.' He shrugs and looks my way briefly. 'Soon after, purely by chance, I ran into one of her close friends and she didn't have a clue what I meant when I mentioned Sofia's recovery. I realised she'd lied about everything to win me back. That was eight months ago. Now she claims she has suspected bowel cancer. She's cried wolf once – I don't know whether to believe her this time.'

'So that night we met in the cocktail bar... the call you got? And at the book fair? All those missed calls I saw on your phone?'

He nods. 'She always sounds so distressed, so convincing. I don't love her in that way anymore, but I do care about her, and I wouldn't be able to live with myself if it was true this time and I just callously abandoned her. It's a mess.'

He grimaces and I feel awful for him. Not only does he have his ex-wife's emotional manipulations to deal with but now he's become embroiled in my problems too. I tell him as much.

He looks over at me with kind eyes and puts one hand on my thigh. 'It's not our fault we're too kind and trusting for our own good, Paige. I'm going to go and have it out with Sofia once and for all – today, as soon as I've dropped you off. I'm not claiming any of it is going to be easy, but I already think it'll be worth it. Us, I mean.'

I take his hand and squeeze it. I think it'll be worth it too.

Chapter Thirty-One

I knock on James's door. It's the first time I've ever been to his house – a handsome mid-terrace just around the corner from the main street in Hessle – and I'm full of nervous anticipation. I imagine Sofia flinging open the door territorially and slapping me across the face for stealing the man she still considers her husband. Or James telling me that he's sorry, but the cancer story is true, and he's decided to stay with her, their love renewed in the face of true tragedy.

However, he opens the door, guides me inside and greets me with a soft peck on the lips, which is promising, unless it's a kiss goodbye. He looks weary and sad, and I steel myself for whatever he might say, pretending that if it all ends here and now, I would be all right. Except I'm not sure he'll be so easy to get over. Given everything that's happened these past few weeks, it would be understandable if I had lost my ability to judge goodness in others, but I now truly feel that he is one of the good ones and I really don't want to lose him.

'Come through,' he says, leading the way through the small, colourful lounge to his kitchen at the back of the house. He rounds the U-shaped counter to make us drinks. It's not on the same scale as Sylvie's but it is a warm and welcoming open-plan kitchen, dining and living space – exposed brick, lots of plants, a log burner, and textured cushions and rugs in burnt oranges and dark greys. It looks like a proper grown-up's home. I want to ask if this is the house he shared with Sofia or the one he moved to after they split, but I resist the temptation to force the moment. He'll tell me in his own time.

Red jumps up from her spot on the fluffy rug within the seating area and scampers over to me excitedly. I haven't brought Hardy with me as I wasn't sure how long I'd be staying. James has arranged for Kenny and Lloyd to meet us here but if he tells me he's chosen Sofia, I know I'll want to leave immediately. I fuss Red affectionately as I surreptitiously watch James making our coffees, drinking in his strong frame and easy movements while I have the chance to.

He takes our drinks over to the settee and invites me to sit down with him. I perch on the edge – coat still on – and look at him as Red settles down at his feet. He reaches down to stroke her as I jiggle my knee anxiously, which he stills with his other hand. Hope and fear jostle within me as I wait expectantly for his news.

'It's over,' he says, and the hope swiftly withers and dies, like one of those time-lapse videos at double speed, over before you realise what you've watched. We're done. He's going back to Sofia. She must have been telling the truth this time. I'm surprised at the force of the emotion within me, the crushing sense of loss at yet another chance at happiness that hasn't worked out. I look away from him and nod too much, not wanting to make a scene although I'm screaming inside.

'Right,' I manage stiffly, still nodding, looking at the mugs on the coffee table. I wonder why he bothered making us drinks. Did he really think I'd stay and have a friendly chat after telling me we were finished?

'Paige?' he questions, ducking his head to meet my eyes, his hand still on my knee. 'I thought you might be pleased?'

'Pleased?' I frown at him, my confusion seemingly matching his.

'It's over,' he repeats. His own concerned expression melts away and he grins, obviously realising I've misunderstood. He spells it out for me. 'Not us. I mean my marriage to Sofia is over.'

'Really?' My bottom lip trembles like a child's on the verge of a meltdown due to overwhelm.

He nods, smiling widely this time, pulling me to him. I breathe him in as I nuzzle into his neck, his strong arms circling me tightly, the tears finally spilling over, from relief, from happiness. He's chosen me.

He tells me everything they said verbatim, understanding my need for frank honesty. He ashamedly admits he called her bluff; told her he'd made an appointment with a specialist he'd researched for a second opinion. She wouldn't commit to going, wouldn't entertain him accompanying her to any of her other supposed appointments either. He pushed her on it until she finally admitted her lie. Although he suspected it, it was still a shock she could be so sly. He told her he couldn't love someone who had abused his trust like she had. He expected her to put up a fight but instead she quietly agreed to the divorce, finally remorseful of her wicked actions, realising she'd gone too far this time.

'I felt like I was in a room with a stranger,' he continues. 'I've known her, loved her, for years, yet most of our relationship has been based on lies, on manipulated feelings. What kind of person does that?'

We look at each other and he sighs. We both know the kinds of people who do things like that.

'The sad thing is, if she hadn't tried to force me or guilt me into staying with her, I would have probably stayed anyway. I didn't love her *because* of her fake illnesses; I loved her in spite of them. She didn't trust me enough to believe that. I forgive her for what she's done, and I kind of understand her screwed-up reasons for doing it, but I won't ever forget such terrible, deliberate lies.'

'How did you leave things?' I ask.

'She was upset... well, that's an understatement, really. It was awful to see. I called her friend – the one I ran into after the tumour story – and she came to be with her. She was as bewildered as me, but we'll make sure Sofia gets help. I won't just abandon her, but she understands it's definitely over between us.'

'You're a good man, James Locksley,' I say. 'Not many of them about, in my experience.'

'Your experience is about to change,' he promises before kissing me again, properly, passionately.

Kenny and Lloyd arrive together shortly afterwards, their curiosity palpable. James greets them and herds them inside as Red spins and dances around them, joyful at the prospect of yet more attention. They oblige her and she sits, basking in their strokes and ear rubs while James makes us all more drinks. I thank them for coming and once James joins us, we begin the story we need them to hear, albeit condensed.

Both men listen intently, and I can see remnants of Kenny's long-shed police demeanour resurface. He asks insightful questions, nodding to simultaneously acknowledge and log my answers. I'm grateful for his seriousness. Lloyd wears a sympathetic then a shocked expression, especially when we reveal Joy's rumourmongering. I think I see a sliver of disappointment in there too, which cements my suspicion that he secretly had a soft spot for her, despite his disdain about her writing "tripe". Well, we all did.

'What can I do to help?' asks Kenny as we finish bringing them up to date with proceedings.

'What can we both do to help?' Lloyd signals between them and I feel overwhelmed by their immediate kindness given my misguided suspicions of the whole group of late. Yet they understand the reasons behind them. It salves my soul to be in the presence of such decent people and I suddenly feel quite emotional. James notices and takes my hand.

'One, we need to know if there's a way to find this motley band of plagiarists and two, if there's a way to prove they've stolen Paige's book,' James states, extending thumb then finger to mark each point.

'You mentioned meeting this Aydan Keyes at a property auction,' says Kenny to James. 'Might they have a record of the lot he bought – could that be where they're currently living?'

James and I look at each other, amazed at how quickly Kenny's detective brain joined dots we'd not even considered.

I want to propel myself at Kenny and hug him, already so thankful to have a starting point to work from. Instead, I settle for a heartfelt smile as James says, 'Wow, great thinking, Detective Inspector Law. It's a possibility, for sure. I might even have that particular auction catalogue stashed somewhere in my files. I'll dig it out for the address.'

'Once you do, let me have it and I'll put a call in to some old colleagues. Suggest a home visit may be in everyone's best interests. Go from there.' Kenny nods at me and bestows me with one of his rare, brief smiles.

'Thank you,' I say to both of them, overcome with gratitude as I squeeze James's hand.

Lloyd puffs out his cheeks and shakes his head, still clearly processing the information. 'I just can't believe it, but it all makes sense now: the rumours, the bitchiness disguised as concern for you. I'm shocked at the way Joy deceived us all so easily. I thought she was a bit on the eccentric side, harmless though. Fun, even. But yes, of course I'm willing to help too. I'll get in touch with my old publishing contacts about the legal ramifications of plagiarism. It was never possible in the traditionally published arena because everything was so heavily vetted but now the independent publishing revolution has shaken everything up. Sadly, according to what I've read recently, author scams are rife.'

'Really?' I ask, hope fading. Why didn't I know this already?

He nods vigorously. 'I've been keeping a close eye on it all, assuming that I would probably have no choice but to publish my next book myself. Forewarned is forearmed and all that. Apparently, the whole industry is contaminated with "black hat teams" – anonymous authors who pay ghostwriters pennies to write a production line of cheap novels which are then published under pseudonyms, sometimes copying passages or whole pages directly from the original authors' books to satisfy the high demand. Then, plagiarists plead ignorance, blaming the ghostwriters for misconstruing their instructions, or their editors or proofreaders for not checking carefully enough and alerting them to the problem. And that's only if they get caught – there are probably plenty who don't,' Lloyd explains.

'In that case, this isn't a case of just plagiarism, is it? It's also fraud – they've stolen all my words and are selling them as their own,' I say.

'Unfortunately, all Amazon requires is a tick in a box to confirm it's your book before it's uploaded and live,' states Lloyd. 'Hopefully, in the future there'll be more rigorous checks in place but right now, it's often just a case of your word against theirs unless you can categorically prove it's your intellectual property, which would probably involve legal representation.'

I hang my head. 'I can't afford that and how can I fight them anyway if I can't even find them? For all I know, Aydan and Joy might not even be their real names.'

'I'm sorry you're having to deal with this, Paige,' sympathises Lloyd. 'I'll find out what else I can and let you know as soon as I do.'

'Thank you both,' I say, as we all stand up. 'I appreciate it so much.'

'Are you going to tell everyone else?' asks Lloyd.

'Yes, at the next meeting on Wednesday, which will be held here,' I confirm. 'As humiliating as all this is for me, I want everyone in the writing group to know the truth.'

Chapter Thirty-Two

'Hello, young man!' I hear Sylvie's voice as she and Renee arrive. 'Oh, what a lovely home, is it all yours?' she asks rudely, passing James the travelling cafetière, obviously prying into his house ownership status and, by definition, his general success.

He laughs, used to her "standard Sylvie" ways by now. 'Yes, it's all mine. Welcome to my humble abode,' he says, placing the cafetière on the granite kitchen counter. 'And we won't be needing this... I've got one of those fancy coffee machines – anyone for a cappuccino or a latte?'

'Ooh, yes please,' says Renee, her eyes practically lighting up. 'I bet Joy will have one too when she gets here.'

James and I exchange a glance as he begins to prepare Renee's drink.

'Actually, I'll just stick to the filter coffee, if you don't mind – I'm a creature of habit,' Sylvie says.

'Me too,' pipes up Kenny from the sofa, Red and Hardy both lying at his feet.

'And me,' adds Lloyd.

I feel strangely comforted by this, by being surrounded by

creatures of habit. I've certainly had my share of the unexpected and there's nothing I want more than to be around honest, reliable, authentic people.

Once everyone is assembled, I nervously announce I have something to say, to explain to all of them.

'Are we not waiting for Joy?' asks Sylvie, craning her neck towards the door as though our missing member is going to burst through it any second, tinkling her apologies for being late, gracing us all with her fun, false persona.

James, Kenny, Lloyd and I look at each other as Sylvie and Renee frown, flummoxed by our silence.

'No,' I confirm. 'You'll understand why very soon.' Then I shakily begin, letting it all pour out, even some of the parts I neglected to tell Kenny and Lloyd on Monday.

'Before I moved here, I was in a relationship with a man named Shane. It was a whirlwind romance, and he proposed after only a few months. After our engagement, he changed dramatically. He manipulated me, he emotionally, physically and sexually abused me, he cheated on me, and he fooled me in the worst way possible. At first, I couldn't prove any of it because he was so adept at lying and covering his tracks.'

I look over at James and he nods and smiles, willing me on. I take a shaky breath and continue.

'I stayed with him for far too long, ashamed of my poor judgement and of the situation I believed I somehow had a hand in creating. I'd already moved in with him and then I left my well-paid job at a newspaper in favour of a lowly admin job near his house, at his request. I became... invisible. Some days, the only reason I had for getting up in the mornings was Hardy. Shane had given me him as a birthday present before things went sour and used him to keep me under control too. I was at absolute rock bottom with no idea how to help myself escape.'

As I gather momentum, I notice that everyone is listening intently, without interruption, even Sylvie.

'Anyway, finally, a way out presented itself. The house was raided early one morning. A team of police seized Shane's computers under the suspicion of him grooming teenage boys through online games. One of the female detectives gave me her card. As soon as Shane returned from being questioned by the police, he stormed out again to find solace in someone else and lick his supposed wounds. He clearly hadn't been charged with anything though and I was mystified – police don't usually raid houses without good reason.'

Kenny nods his agreement at this.

'So, I rang the detective and told her he must have another computer somewhere and gave her the names I could remember seeing on his screen and any ex-girlfriends he'd mentioned. She said they'd be keeping an eye on him, searching the computers they'd already seized again and would keep me updated. I had no choice but to go and live with my grandad – a vicious, dying drunk with liver disease. The only saving grace was that Shane didn't even know I had a grandad as I'd told him he'd died. I was ashamed of lying at the time – wishful thinking on my part perhaps – but I was so glad I had. Anyway, a couple of weeks later I heard back from that detective. Evidence of Shane grooming a teenage boy was found on another computer he owned that he kept at one of his two girlfriend's houses. She also had a teenage son.'

Sylvie and Renee both gasp with shock.

'I stayed with my grandad and became his carer, despite what he put me through after my parents died. After he died too, I used nearly every penny I inherited from his house sale to buy my house here, in Hull, to make a fresh start. I never looked back – I began my proofreading business, joined this writing group and even met a new boyfriend, Aydan. For the first time in a very long time, I had hope. You all inspired me to write, and I wrote a novel based on my experiences.'

'So, *Descent into Deceit* is about you and this Shane?' asks Renee, joining the dots.

'It's a novel but yes, large chunks of it are wholly autobiographical,' I confirm. Sylvie places a palm to her chest but doesn't comment. 'For weeks now, I've had a horrible feeling of being watched and strange things have been happening.' I pause to harness the courage to admit what I need to say next. 'I could feel my mental health beginning to regress. I became jumpy and paranoid and suspicious all over again, but of myself this time. I'm ashamed to say that I thought one of you, or Alexander, stole my manuscript at the book fair. I was convinced one of you wanted to steal my book for yourselves.' I look at Renee apologetically.

'I can understand why you thought that about Alexander, Paige,' reassures Renee, softly. 'I assume you're going to tell us you know it wasn't him though? He's a sod at times but he's not a thief.'

'I know,' I reply. I cast my gaze around the whole group. 'It wasn't any of you here today, but it was Joy – Aydan's mother.'

Sylvie and Renee's hands fly to their faces in shock, as though synchronised.

James walks over, sits on the arm of the chair next to me and takes my hand. Sylvie and Renee both register the significance but remain wide-eyed and quiet as I continue.

'It gets worse, if you can believe that? Aydan and Shane are in a relationship now. Joy has known Shane since he was a young boy; he's a couple of years older than Aydan. Joy initially took him under her wing after her husband ran off with Shane's mother and considers him a second son, yet she still gave their relationship her blessing. They've all been working together to get revenge for everything they believe I "did" to Shane.'

'You mean phoning the police detective?' asks Renee. 'But that was the right thing to do!'

'Not just that,' I say. 'A few weeks before the police raid, I saw an old journalist colleague of mine, Julia, in a coffee shop. I was in a bad way, physically and mentally. Like all reporters, she could see right through my lies, yet I refused her offers of help, afraid of the repercussions. A few days after I left Shane, I got in touch with her too and finally told her the truth about him and the police search. She printed the story in the local paper apparently. It forced Shane out of his house and into hiding, with Joy and Aydan. But then he was caught. They came up with their plan to ruin me then, as revenge for ruining Shane's life, while he was serving his prison sentence. They all orchestrated my demise and stole my manuscript. It's currently for sale on Amazon, under their pen name, apparently selling well.'

'Can a debut novel written by an unknown author make that much money, to make it worth their while to do all this?' asks Renee. 'I mean, we all know how hard it is to get sales.' Kenny and Lloyd nod their agreement.

'Aydan's a marketing whizz, apparently – knows his stuff about ads and promos. And they're in it for the long haul so they'll wring as much out of it as they can. They've achieved their main goal, which is to hurt me.'

Sylvie shakes her head in disbelief and flings her hands in the air dramatically, reminding me, sadly, of Joy. 'You couldn't write this!' she states.

'Plot twists galore,' quips Lloyd, throwing a sympathetic smile my way.

I sigh heavily. 'There's more yet...'

Chapter Thirty-Three

'At the weekend Aydan took me on a supposed break to the Lake District, still under the guise of being my boyfriend,' I continue. 'They arranged that Shane and Joy would ambush me there, which they did. Shane threatened me and Hardy. He said that if I go to the police or try to prove he's fraudulently selling my book, he'd hurt us.'

'And Joy is really in on all this?' asks Renee, eyes wide, incredulous.

'She's been playing us all,' interjects James. 'The cheerful eccentric is just an act. She spread nasty rumours about Paige within this group to undermine her and they're planning on stealing other authors' manuscripts now that they've hit on a profitable con. Her erotic novels were probably stolen from another author too,' he tells the group.

Sylvie and Renee shift in their seats, glancing at each other, clearly trying to process all the shocking information I've shared so far.

'Anyway,' I say, 'we don't know where they are now, and apparently it's really difficult to prove your book has been plagiarised or stolen if you're an independent author.' I look over at Lloyd who nods his confirmation. 'Lloyd's going to do a bit more research and ask around for me and I'm looking into what I can do about Shane's intimidation and threats, but I don't mind admitting I'm scared of the repercussions. I just want him to stay in the past, for good this time.'

'And you two...' Renee asks, signalling to mine and James's clasped hands.

James looks at me and smiles. 'A little while,' he admits, skirting neatly over the specifics.

'James rescued me,' I share. 'In the Lakes. He helped me when I needed him most and I couldn't be more grateful.'

'Joy actually told us you were married, James – is that true or another of her lies?' Sylvie asks with an arched brow, always one to remember details.

'Things have been...' He frowns, searching for the most appropriate description of our situations. He finally settles on, 'Complicated. Now you know Paige's story, but I had difficulties of my own too, in my marriage.'

I see a flash of disapproval cross Sylvie's face. He sees it too.

'My wife Sofia and I separated – for the second time – a few months ago. She's another liar, unfortunately. She lied about being seriously ill twice to win me back, but things have gone too far and now we're over for good.'

'Lied about being seriously ill?' asks Kenny, eyebrows raised.

James nods. 'Last time she claimed she had a tumour, which was fictitious, and this time she claimed she was having tests for suspected cancer.'

'Wow,' comments Lloyd with an exaggerated blink and Sylvie's expression changes from disapproval back to shock. I squeeze James's hand in support.

'Well, in the spirit of sharing, I should probably come clean about what's really going on with Alexander,' says Renee.

I lean forward, interested in hearing what Renee has to say.

James's hand moves to rest on my back, and I feel comforted and supported by his touch.

Renee tucks her frizzy mane behind her ears, swallows and begins to speak. 'We adopted Alexander when he was three after years of infertility heartbreak. He was a challenging child, but we were so overjoyed to finally be parents that we indulged him. It was obvious he was extremely bright from a young age but throughout his school years he became progressively more arrogant and condescending, which meant he didn't make friends. That in turn alienated Geoff and I as he was never invited to play dates or parties or sleepovers, not that he ever seemed bothered. But we were – it broke our hearts.' She shrugs, her expression sad as she stares at Red and Hardy lying peacefully on the rug together.

'He had a promising future at university but became... troubled. He attempted an overdose, which he survived, but then he dropped out. He was self-aware enough to realise his superior intelligence yet oblivious to the negative effect he had on others. Of course, we blamed ourselves for all of it, which put a huge strain on our marriage. Geoff and I now support him emotionally and financially. We were both planning on an early retirement, perhaps go on a few holidays, but that can't happen yet. Alexander thinks we're suffocating him, that we're stopping him from returning to university, but we'd love him to be independent again, when he's well enough. The phrase Geoff keeps using is "resentful but resilient". What else can we do? He's our son.' She presses her lips together and blinks rapidly, obviously trying to suppress the emotion she feels. We all murmur comments of sympathy and support, and she nods her thanks.

That explains Alexander's outburst at the book fair about his mum being a liar, I think, which I still choose not to share with Renee. I feel so sorry for her and her husband. Alexander too.

'I don't know how resilient I am,' Lloyd pipes up. He sighs heavily, hands clasped together, one thumb stroking the other nervously. 'I've been weighed down with my own problems all these years yet what you've all been through...'

'Mate, no one is less valid than anyone else,' James reassures him. 'Tell us what happened, if you want to.'

Lloyd gives James a tight smile then puckers his lips, obviously deliberating whether or not to offload. He decides to. 'I was first published over a decade ago. After years of teaching maths, I wrote a textbook and patented a new piece of equipment to go with it, for reading graphs. They really took off and sold well, enough to leave teaching and write full time for a while. So, I wrote a similar second book, but my heart wasn't in it. It did okay but had nowhere near the success of the first one, so my two-book contract wasn't renewed. After that, the plan was to pour all my efforts into the literary novel I always wanted to write, but it never happened. I got lazy and demotivated, frittered most of the money away. My marriage collapsed and I was forced to go back to agency supply teaching; a washed-up author returning to the day job.' He chuckles without mirth.

'I was bitter and furious with myself. I couldn't teach – seeing my patented design in use in the classrooms was a never-ending reminder of the success I couldn't maintain, but I couldn't write any more either, not even another textbook; I couldn't get past the brain block. I got signed off with depression after a few months and was referred for counselling.'

'Did it help?' I ask, feeling a surge of sympathy.

Lloyd considers his answer for a moment. 'Not as much as this group, actually. Being around other writers again made me feel like I could give it another go, so I did. Paige, I'm sorry for believing Joy over you and dropping you as my proofreader, but

I'm proud of myself for having another go, which is something I didn't think I'd be able to do again.'

'Apology accepted,' I say, and we smile at each other.

Lloyd refills his cup from the cafetière dregs on the coffee table, then pulls a face as he realises it's gone cold. He puts his cup back down as Kenny clears his throat, obviously preparing to share his tale too. I think I know what he's going to talk about, and I feel humbled that he trusts us enough to share it.

'I'm not much of a public speaker these days,' he begins, 'but I think I'd like to tell you a story too, if that's all right with everybody?'

We all nod and verbalise our encouragement, and I've no doubt that every one of us appreciates this safe space.

Kenny clears his throat again. 'It was a normal Tuesday night. Alice – my wife – was out at her usual book club a few streets away. She never came home. I went out looking for her and saw her umbrella in the road before I saw the ambulance. I remember thinking she'd be furious her hair was getting wet.' He gives a half laugh as Sylvie softly gasps, her hand over her chest once more.

'The worst part was telling our daughter in Australia, not being able to tell her face to face that her mum was killed in a hit-and-run–' His voice catches and he stops, making a conscious effort to compose himself. Renee reaches over to place a supporting hand on his arm, and he pats it gratefully.

'Anyway,' he continues, choking back his memories, 'this group has given me a new lease of life; a reason to go on. Alice would have loved to see me writing again. Before this group it had been thirty years since I'd put pen to any paper that wasn't an official police document.'

'You were in the police?' asks Renee.

'Detective Inspector Law.' Kenny smiles with pride. 'But after Alice... they caught the driver, but he got off with a fine. I lost all faith in the system I'd served in for decades. I took early retirement, downsized the house and tried to figure out where I fitted in the world. I'm not ashamed to say I was a bit lost – no wife, and a daughter living on the other side of the world. Like you can clearly all identify with, it was a difficult time. But, onwards and upwards, as they say, and I'm pleased to have finally found a little piece of creative enjoyment again.' He nods once as if to punctuate the end of his story.

My heart swells with sympathy for him, and for the whole motley bunch of us. People really do experience some terrible things yet make it through somehow, forever changed but still hopeful for a new version of happiness.

'Well, as we're all sharing, I suppose it wouldn't hurt to throw my hat in the ring too, as it were, although my tale isn't nearly as tall as some of yours,' Sylvie says as though she is put out by the fact that we've outdone her somehow with our woes. James and I share a wry smile.

'Simply put, my husband divorced me, many years ago,' she states. 'There was nothing as dramatic as another woman – as far as I know – or a secret revealed, or any other tempestuous circumstances. He casually announced he didn't want to be married to me anymore and so he left. Just like that. I never saw him again after that day, the solicitors dealt with everything. To be fair, the divorce settlement was very generous on his part as I had always worked as a homemaker whilst we were married.'

In my mind's eye I'm reminded of Miss Havisham, an abandoned woman living in lonely luxury.

'There's been no one since.' Her lips tighten but her chin raises as though in a gesture of strength, despite her obvious sadness. 'My husband worked all hours – he ran a successful building company, so I was alone a lot anyway. I got used to it. He didn't even give me a child to keep me company.' After a second her expression softens slightly. 'After he left, I read even more voraciously, mostly romantic and fairy-tale fantasy, the elusive happy ever after. I loved being lost in those stories; they were classic escapism. Then one day I thought I would give it a go myself – write the life, the happy marriage I wish I'd had.'

'Oh, Sylvie,' says Renee.

'Water under the bridge now,' she says matter-of-factly. 'Right, I'll make myself useful, if you don't mind, James. Anyone for more coffee?'

'Can I have tea?' I ask. 'Now that we're being honest, I actually hate filter coffee.'

Chapter Thirty-Four

April 2017

I'm drinking tea at James's house and Hardy and Red are snoozing on the rug in the shafts of spring sunlight streaming through his open bi-fold doors. It's gorgeous to see them lying so contentedly together. The birds are chirping and the smell of freshly cut grass wafts into the house from the Tower Hill communal green outside.

James is out – he's gone to view another potential portfolio property – but he insisted I stay here with the dogs, to enjoy a leisurely Saturday morning. I wonder briefly if Sofia ever sat here, like me, drinking tea and waiting for his return, but I quickly banish the thought from my mind. I might not be great at banishing everything, but I'm secure enough in the way James feels about me to not allow comparisons with his ex-wife to burrow into my brain as frequently. After everything, I'm grateful for, and appreciative of, the calm and the quiet. I return to thinking about recent events, turning them over, back to front and upside down in my head, like a tongue constantly ferreting out a newly empty tooth socket.

It's been a few days since our writing group revelations and some progress has already been made. Unfortunately, Lloyd's knowledge regarding the plagiarism is secure – I don't really have a leg to stand on unless I want to take them to court, which I can't do as I can't prove anything concrete. I have emailed Amazon to report my stolen book though, but there's been no response as yet. As I suspected, it's probably a case of my word against theirs but at least I'm trying to fight it.

However, on a more positive note, Kenny advised me I could press historic assault charges and file a protection order against Shane, even without knowing where he is, which I have done. Now that the protection order is in place, I do rest a bit easier, but that's partly due to James. We haven't spent a night apart since the last group meeting and we're slowly getting to know each other properly after our dramatic revelations. What a way to start a relationship!

My phone, beside me on the sofa, vibrates with an email alert. Neither dog stirs and I smile at their furry forms, envying their constantly carefree lives. The email is from Julia. James suggested I confidentially contact my old journalist friend and colleague who wrote the police raid story in the newspaper after I left Shane. So, when I woke in the early hours from another nightmare reliving my time with him, I emailed her, the whole updated story pouring out of me. I pressed send before I could regret my honesty. But I've been fretting about it ever since, my old vulnerability and shame returning with force, annoyed at myself for offering up such a clickbait story more than readily. I suddenly feel exhausted with it all – will Shane always dominate my life like this, even when he's not around? How can I ever sever our contaminated connection?

I open Julia's message, preparing to be informed that some clause or other determines she can publish what she likes.

> Paige, it's so good to hear from you!
> I've tried contacting you so many

times these past months, but I suspected you had changed your number and email address. Well done you for getting out of that situation and being strong enough to stay away from him before the story went live. I was worried about you staying regardless, but I should have known you were made of braver stuff than that, despite everything he did to you. I suspected foul play before you left The Gazette, and that time I saw you I felt sure he was abusing you, but you kept it all to yourself. I'm glad you trusted me enough to tell me about the police raid though. It all became clear exactly the kind of man he was very quickly. He deserved the repercussions he got — karma is a bitch!

As you know, there were a few calls to the news desk after the story was published — two ex-girlfriends reported a similar history with him and one had a young son whose behaviour changed dramatically while she was with Shane. She was distraught for not coming forward herself sooner. I put her in touch with a counsellor after informing the police what she said.

You might not know that there were a couple of people who claimed they had seen him skulking round playgrounds and the secondary school gates too. The community turned on him — spray-painted his house, smashed the windows, posted faeces through the letter box, the usual. Not saying I agree with vigilante justice, but our job is to report the news and keep people informed and they deserved to know what he was being investigated for. Sadly, he still hadn't been charged at that point, but it was enough for him to go into hiding. Thankfully, justice was served in the end when he did go down, and the house was sold not long after, for a knock-down price of course.

I'm so sorry he's still torturing you, and the fact that he's recruited people to help him is outrageous! You've really been through it, haven't you? I'll do absolutely anything I can to help — get me proof and I'll run it as a story, or I'll be a witness, if you ever need one. Until then, please feel reassured that everything you've told me remains completely confidential.

Good luck with getting back what is rightfully yours!

Take care — I mean it.

Julia

I close my eyes and rest my head back on the sofa cushion. I'm vibrating with validation and feel lucky to have escaped relatively unscathed in the grand scheme of things. I can't imagine how worried the woman with the son must have been. Our stories belong in those trashy real-life magazines: *I fell for a charming, child-grooming abuser!* But he's still at it — lying, threatening, stealing, manipulating, seeking revenge for his supposed injustices. A man like that will never change. He's incapable of it. But he needs to be stopped, and if I've done it once, I can do it again. Like Julia says, I need to find proof.

Chapter Thirty-Five

I let myself in to my dark, silent house and bend down to collect the few bits of junk mail puddled on my doormat, pushing the door closed with my heel. It feels strange to be here after a few days away ensconced at James's house – us and the dogs cohabitating happily. Hardy's still there while I've popped back home. Unlike Shane, James can be trusted with my precious pooch.

I found out that his house is not the one he shared with Sofia, it's his alone. She still lives in their old one, although no longer at James's expense. She's now claiming she's going to start applying for jobs and he's hoping it means she's finally turned a corner in her Munchausen syndrome recovery.

I turn the light on then flick through the flyers and the local magazine and see there is also a missed parcel notification, although I don't remember ordering anything. I plonk them all on the bottom step before running upstairs to empty and repack my bag for another couple of nights at James's house. As if he can read my mind, he texts my brand-new phone:

> Ordering the takeaway now… what do you fancy? Xxx

I smile as I imagine the scene that awaits me when I return: James sitting on his sofa, laptop balanced on his legs, feet up on the coffee table creating a bridge over the warm, furry bodies of Hardy and Red.

> Apart from you? 😉 Nothing too spicy - you choose. I'll be back in half an hour. Xxx

A few minutes later, just as I'm about to leave, I remember the parcel notification slip and check again where they've left it – over the side gate. I hope whatever it is isn't damaged after being dropped from that height. I unlock the back door and wave my arm for the security light to come on, but the bulb must be out because the tiny backyard remains shrouded in darkness. I tut then scoot round the side path to collect it, feeling around blindly until my hands make contact with the cardboard box.

Back inside, I tear open the perforated seal and yank out the contents which I immediately drop as though scalded. There, lying on my kitchen floor, is my missing manuscript.

I recoil from it, edging slowly backwards, as though it's a bomb about to explode. I'm gasping for breath, head and heart pounding with fear of this inanimate object because of what I know it means. He knows where I am and he's coming for me.

'Hello, Paige. Good of you to finally make an appearance. I've been waiting for you.'

I whirl round, absolute panic gripping me in its tight, meaty fist as I struggle to comprehend the sight before me. His frame seems to fill the back doorway, and he's silhouetted against the dark living room beyond, just like the stereotypical bad guy in a suspense movie. Time seems to suspend as our entire history spools through my brain like a freaky cinematic montage, ending with the memory of him cruelly clutching Hardy's snout at the Lakes. I am filled with absolute hate and absolute fear. His smirk revolts me, his face disgusts me, yet I am frozen to the spot with my phone in my eyeline, right there on the worktop, nearer to him than me.

'I've got a protection order against you,' I say bravely yet pointlessly.

He rolls his eyes as he huffs out an amused breath. He casually removes his cap and then lunges for me, grabbing my hair. I'm not deft enough to dodge him, seemingly out of practice. He twists my hair around his hand and yanks my head back with such force my throat closes, and I can't breathe. I desperately claw at him, aware of him laughing as he punches me in my side with his other fist, his old favourite move. He lets go of my hair as I crumple to the kitchen floor, curling into the foetal position, arms protectively circled around my head.

He squats down next to me, arms casually draped over his knees as if to address a disobedient pet. 'What did I warn you about, eh?' he asks conversationally.

I don't respond; it's better to not respond.

'I warned you not to defy me, didn't I? I was very clear, wasn't I, Paige? I gave you one chance – a ticket to oblivion. I warned you to just let it lie, but you couldn't, could you?'

I concentrate on breathing as he continues with his indulgent monologue.

'You don't deserve oblivion anyway, and you certainly don't deserve to be a success because you didn't even work for it. It was all me.' He jabs a finger at his chest. 'I inspired you, inspired your book, inspired you to play at being Little Miss Author, telling tales, just for fun. And that's all they are, you know – tall tales. I was wrongly convicted thanks to you and that other whore I was stringing along too. Both lying little bitches.

Considering what a fucking timid little mouse you were throughout our joke of a relationship, you suddenly had a lot to say at the end, which funnily enough, coincided with me losing the last shred of interest I still had in you.'

He's leaning down close to my ear now; I can practically hear the venom escaping through the tiny gaps in his gritted teeth.

'Well, mice don't belong in the limelight, they belong in a cage, and that's where you'll stay when I've finished with you, tightly contained in your small, insignificant surroundings while I soar in the glory of freedom and success. Remember, you're pathetic. You're insignificant. You're nothing but a blank Paige.'

He's using the same insult he used in the Lakes, his supposedly clever play on words. I'm trying to block him out – this isn't happening, this isn't happening – but I hear him ordering me to get up. I'm cocooned inside my own head, eyes screwed shut, humming. Anything to make it all go away.

'I knew I should have fucked you over sooner, as soon as I found out where you were, but Aydan talked me out of it,' he deigns to explain.

I try to squash my body into the floor, praying for the ground to somehow open and suck me down into its depths, transport me somewhere, anywhere, out of his reach.

'Not because he had any fucking feelings for you,' he hisses, anticipating my thought process. 'But because he was protecting me.' He jabs himself in the chest again to reinforce his point.

'He thought I'd been through enough – thanks to your handiwork with the local rag and then doing time. It was his idea to play the long game; he's actually much more devious than I originally gave him credit for. Then when Joy joined us, it became even more fun, watching you disintegrate before our eyes. Way more effective and enjoyable than just hunting you down. But you had to go and make more trouble, didn't you?'

He sighs dramatically at my continued non-compliance of his demand and pulls me up from the floor by my hair again. I yelp in pain. I hear my phone vibrate but again, I can't get to it. He pushes me forcefully through to the living room and closes the door behind us, leaning his bulk back against it, ankles and arms crossed, appraising me. Tears are coursing down my face but I'm silent, defiant and full of gratitude that Hardy isn't here. Horrific images of what could have happened flash through my mind, and I crush my eyelids shut against them.

'I forgot to say in the Lakes that you're looking well,' he compliments, completely changing tack. 'You got a bit too chubby when we were together but you're getting your slender lines back now. Good for you.'

My eyes snap open – I need my wits about me – as I defensively cross my arms against my chest, my hand pressed against my side due to the throbbing pain from Shane's punch. It feels tender and hot, just like all those times before, but at least it's bearable, not like the agony of a broken rib.

'Aydan says he thinks you look all right naked. I always thought so too.'

I blush fiercely, humiliation and anger dancing together, but I remain quiet.

'And now you've got a new one on the go – you don't waste any time, do you? Does your current fella know you're damaged goods?'

He takes a step closer to me and I take a step back, edging closer to the fireplace behind me. I glance around, briefly amazed at the unfamiliarity of my own home, suddenly a danger zone.

'Hmm?' he prompts. 'Does your new bloke know he's fucking a damaged little whore?' His expression belies his question; he could be asking me for directions such is the incongruity of his mask. 'A dirty little simpering whore who picks up men wherever she goes, and all they have to do to get her into bed is to flatter her a little bit, pay the little mouse a teeny bit of attention. Easy-peasy fucking pie. Does he know you like it rough sometimes?'

I shake my head vigorously as I wipe my tears and running nose with the heel of my hand, nervously anticipating his next move and desperately praying it's not what I think it might be. He's another step closer now and as a result my back is pressed against the chimney-breast wall.

He laughs and clucks his tongue. 'No, he doesn't know, or no, you don't like it rough anymore?'

I stare at him, trembling, lips pressed together, forcing myself to keep breathing and stay strong. I'm standing as upright as I can manage given the pain I'm in, but he still lurches above me. He's so close I can smell his aftershave and the leather of his jacket, smells that used to bring excitement and happiness but now only bring memories I try so hard to forget.

'Get undressed,' he says.

I stare at him, silently refusing, desperate to escape the degrading command by force of will alone.

'Do you realise how badly you fucked my life up?' he screams in my face. I instinctively close my eyelids against the spittle flying from his lips. 'Get. Fucking. Undressed. We're going to have some fun, just like old times.'

Chapter Thirty-Six

Like a pincer, Shane's hand shoots forward and grabs my arm to keep me steady while his other hand tears at the collar of my top, roughly yanking it down over my shoulder. I twist down and scream out simultaneously, trying to turn away from him, but his arm snakes around my waist and he holds me tightly against him. The pain still radiates from where he punched me, the pressure being exerted now increasing it tenfold. I kick against him, but he restrains me, both arms wrapped round me now, clamping my own arms against me so tightly I feel like I'm wearing a weighted straitjacket. I can feel he's hard. I know exactly what he's going to do, and I'm terrified beyond measure, yet my brain is quickly calculating the possible outcomes depending on my next move. He enjoys the struggle. It turns him on more than if I become vacant and submissive – I know this from bitter experience. I go limp. If this surprises or disappoints him he doesn't let on; he's going to go through with it regardless.

He shoves me towards the sofa and knees the back of my legs to make me bend down. He kneels behind me and forces my head down onto the cushions, keeping his hand on the back of my neck. I can hear his ragged breathing and a jangling as his other hand fumbles to undo his belt. He's pressing my face down so hard I can barely catch my breath through the fabric of the sofa, already soggy from my tears. I try to tune out, to take myself away from my body as he pulls down my leggings and knickers, goose pimples pricking my skin despite the relative warmth of the room. As stupid as it sounds, I try not to brace myself, knowing any resistance will just make it so much more painful than it's already going to be...

'Paige!' I hear my name then feel the door between living room and hallway bang against the sofa. All at once Shane releases my neck and jerks away from me as I catch sight of James lurching into the room towards him. A gasping sob escapes me as James punches a still-kneeling Shane with such force that he keels backwards, off-kilter, hands flying up to his wounded face. James pounces forward, like a frenzied animal, and straddles Shane's torso, punching the soft flesh of his stomach, underneath his ribs, his neck, his chin, his face, wherever he can make fist on bone or skin contact between Shane's splayed, defensive hands. He's absolutely insane with fury.

'James!' I cry, pulling up my leggings and crawling over to him, reaching out to touch him, to try to catch his arms somehow. 'Stop, please stop.' I beg him over and over, terrified of the possible consequences of these violent actions, despite feeling overwhelming gratitude that he has prevented worse from happening to me.

He eventually either hears me or runs out of adrenaline. He stops throwing punches. He's panting heavily like a professional boxer end-fight, his knuckles bloodied, his face splashed with sweat and blood. He looks wild-eyed, rabid and spent. He twists towards me and his expression immediately clears and softens, as though an alternative personality has suddenly emerged. I embrace him tightly and I can feel him trembling as I sob uncontrollably into his chest while he murmurs reassurances that I'm going to be okay.

'Is he dead?' I ask, my voice raw and gasping.

James leans down and presses two fingers against Shane's neck, waits for a few seconds. He shakes his head. 'No, he's still alive. I'll call the police and ask for an ambulance too.' He pulls me to him again. 'Thank God you're okay. I had a bad feeling when you were late back and didn't answer your phone. I asked my neighbour to stay with the dogs and rushed straight here.'

In that exact moment, Shane sits up and springs forward, a surprise snake lying in wait for its moment to dart and bite.

I scream in shock, recognising the malicious intent in his eye, the other swollen shut. As the two men fight again, one my abuser, one my protector, I'm a statue, unable to think, to act.

I need to get out.

I somehow propel myself to the kitchen, one clear aim in mind as the soundtrack of punches and grunts continues. They're both strong men; an equal physical match for each other but I'm terrified of Shane's unrelenting sociopathic edge spurring him on beyond his fighting capabilities. He thrives on adrenaline and the desire for control. I snatch a carving knife from the wooden block. I'll do whatever I have to, to save James and to save myself from the monster invading my home and my life.

I sneak back to peer through the doorway and see Shane pull his arm back as though readying a bow and arrow. His clenched fist smashes into James's skull, causing his eyes to roll back in his head. He flops, seemingly unconscious. Shane huffs with exhaustion and spits blood onto James's torso before slowly turning his sights on me. I'm trapped once more. But I'm not helpless, not this time. He advances towards me.

The knife pierces his abdomen with a swooshing sound; it's

almost musical in its beauty. I feel completely at peace as it happens, the hilt making contact with flesh followed by another swooshing note as I withdraw it again. He moans softly and, as you often see in films, looks down at his fresh wound, at the neat slit I've just created in his T-shirt, his skin, at the blood already gushing from it. He looks back at me as I stick the knife in again, higher up, but this time I let go of it, watching, weirdly fascinated, as he rocks unsteadily once, twice, before slumping heavily to the floor. I feel imbued with relief as I stare down at him.

I step over the heap of him and kneel next to James, whispering his name, stroking his face tenderly. Blood bubbles up through his parted lips and I turn him onto his side as he tries to cough. My heavy tears land on his hand as he reaches for me.

I shakily stand up and pull him towards me, away from the meaty, pulpy mess of Shane, now barely recognisable.

The police and ambulance arrive minutes after I call them. The efficient paramedics fire off a few questions while they first package Shane up then cart him off on a stretcher.

I follow as they transport James out to the second ambulance then step into the starkly illuminated interior and sit beside him. The blood covering him seems to glow in the fluorescent light.

'Are you okay?' the paramedic asks.

I nod, still shaking. 'I think I will be now.'

Chapter Thirty-Seven

I feel someone shaking me and I jump with the shock of the touch, immediately grasping my cricked neck. I must have fallen asleep here in the hospital's waiting room. I sit up as the nurse sits down next to me.

'How's James?' I ask, my memory instantaneously filling me in on everything that had happened mere hours before – Shane's intrusion, the attempted rape, the brutal fight...

'He's going to have a hell of a headache when he wakes up but he's going to be fine,' she says, smiling. 'Would you like to see him?'

My face crumples and I nod, tears of relief and exhaustion splashing to the floor as I lean forward and rest my own weary head in my hands, so thankful that James is all right, that Shane didn't destroy him, didn't destroy us.

'What about Shane Kennedy?' I ask.

'As soon as you've seen James, there are two police officers who need to speak with you about Mr Kennedy. They'll be able to fill you in.' She stands, ready to show me the way.

I try to read her expression, but her professionalism masks

any clue. I nod again, wipe my eyes and fall in step with her as she takes me to James.

A little while later, as dawn is beginning to break, two police officers approach the bed. They introduce themselves as Detective Inspector Harrison and Sergeant Singh, apologise for the timing, and ask to speak with me.

'How do you know Mr Kennedy, Miss Carrigan?' DI Harrison asks.

'He's my ex-fiancé. I left him in 2013 but now he's... is he dead?' I ask abruptly.

They exchange a glance then DI Harrison suggests, 'Why doesn't Sergeant Singh get you a cuppa? You look like you could do with one.' Her sergeant nods before disappearing from the room.

'Is Shane dead?' I repeat, suddenly desperate to know.

'He's currently in a critical condition,' DI Harrison confirms. 'We need to ask you a few questions. Is that okay, Paige?'

I stare at her tired and hollow face and wonder if my answers to her questions are going to be typical, if she's going to understand why I did what I did, if I'm eventually going to be charged with murder, or manslaughter, for defending myself against him – a liar, a rapist, an abuser – in my own home. As I stare at her and wonder these things, I realise that no matter what she thinks of me, no matter what happens to me, it was worth it. Stabbing him was worth it.

I nod.

'Okay,' she says, pulling up a chair. 'In your own time and words, could you tell us what happened at your home last night?'

Sergeant Singh returns with a plastic cup of surprisingly strong sweet tea. I accept it gratefully, taking a sip before setting it down on James's bedside table. I gaze at my boyfriend, at his bruised and bleeding face, while thinking about my own mental and physical injuries, my lingering shame and humiliation caused by a very bad man, and the relief that this living nightmare may now all be over.

I take James's hand, take a breath and begin to tell them my story.

Epilogue

April 2018

I gaze around the bookstore. Bunches of beautiful flowers, cupcakes adorned with miniature book toppers and sparkling-wine flutes decorate the circular tables edging the room courtesy of Belinda's brand-new venture: *Belinda Penfold Events*. She's done a great job organising everything; her attention to detail is second to none.

Eadie Lee, an Instagram 'sensation', is interviewing me tonight, here, at my book launch. Once everyone in the surprisingly long queue has been welcomed inside and taken their seats, she introduces me as Paige Carrigan – there's no pen name for me.

'Welcome, Paige.' Her smile sparkles, glittery red lips revealing perfect white teeth. Photogenic is too tame a description for Eadie; her winged eyeliner alone is applied with artistic precision. 'Congratulations on your brand-new novel – *Liar, Liar!* Just in case there might be a few people left who haven't read it yet, what's the book about?'

I gaze around the room at the people assembled, in rows, before me, my social anxiety finally under control in this proud, pinch-me moment. 'It's about a stolen manuscript and a writer's revenge,' I state with a smile. Eadie whoops and the audience laugh, clapping to show their approval.

My imagination conjures up an image of Shane, trapped in his cell, reading the copy I sent him. He's back behind bars for my attempted rape. And thanks to Julia covering the story, as well as Kenny having a word in his ex-police colleagues' ears, another woman and one young man came forward to press charges against him too.

Sadly, I was never able to prove his part in the theft of *Descent Into Deceit* as it mysteriously disappeared off Amazon shortly after Shane was arrested. I'd like to think Aydan and Joy's consciences got the better of them, but who knows? Perhaps they decided to sever themselves from the situation, and Shane, completely. Or maybe they still huddle around a prison visiting table once a fortnight plotting more revenge due to their corrupted allegiance to a rapist and child groomer who seems to have them both fooled. I must admit, though, their mind games and theft of my manuscript paled into insignificance compared to everything else that Shane himself did. I catch myself getting sucked back into the memories and quickly tune back into Eadie.

'Let's answer a few questions,' she suggests. 'We've got five lined up already!'

There's a large screen behind us showing a static image of my book alongside a handful of glowing reviews from fellow authors and book bloggers, which changes to an open, blank book as she speaks. The first question, previously sent in via Instagram, shows up on its pages:

What inspired you to write the book?

'Unfortunately, as some of you may already know, this book is based on a true story. They do say write what you know but I hope not to live through too many more traumatic life events just to write a good book!'

The audience of mainly women laughs at my answer, a few nodding along in agreement.

What tips would you give aspiring writers?

I think for a moment, looking out over the crowd, all eager to hear my answer. 'Join a writing group,' I say. 'Mine was invaluable to me when I wrote my first novel. I had to leave when I moved away but we're still in touch now – well, most of us.'

I can't help but think of Joy, of the person I really liked, the brilliant actress who played her role so well, and wonder where she is now. An erotic trilogy appeared for sale online a few months ago with the same titles and covers she used but under a different author name. I assumed they were hers and I was heartened to read several scathing one-star reviews.

Who did you have in mind when writing your main character – who was your inspiration?

The answer to this question is one I already know. 'My main character is an amalgam of all strong, creative, independent women everywhere. Although I did have a very specific inspiration – myself – I hope that my main character is relatable for all my readers, and I hope the message of the book is that good *always* triumphs over evil.'

The audience responds to this with a few whoops and cheers, and Eadie gives me a wink and a sensational smile, encouraging me to bask in the applause.

Are any aspects of the book truly autobiographical?

I frown and look down, taking comfort in the sight of my engagement and wedding rings. I twizzle them as I answer. 'Sadly, yes, there are aspects of the book which are autobiographical. That is why ten per cent of the royalties from this book will be donated to Domestic Violence UK. If any of the themes in the book trigger or resonate negatively with any reader, I urge them to contact one or more of the helplines listed in the back pages. There are also leaflets on the tables here tonight. Please, do not suffer in silence. If this book helps other people to access the help they need, I'll feel as though I've done something good.'

Are you single?

The mood is lightened, and everyone giggles, including me. 'No, I'm very much taken,' I reply, smoothing my hands over my swollen pregnant belly.

'Shall we take a few personal questions from the audience?' asks sparkly Eadie. I nod my assent, pride and pleasure rippling through me, not least because not so long ago, I wouldn't have been able to attend an event like this, much less be the star of the show, so to speak. It's trite but true: what doesn't kill you makes you stronger.

Hands shoot up.

'I loved this book!' one young woman exclaims. 'Are you writing anything new?'

'Thank you. And actually, I've already written my next book,' I reveal. 'This isn't its first iteration, but it's already been through quite the thorough publication process.'

'Does it have a working title yet?' the girl follows up.

'Yes... it's a prequel to *Liar, Liar!* and it's called *Descent into Deceit.*'

As Eadie expertly and efficiently closes the event,

reminding everyone the interview has been recorded and will be replayed online, a handsome man approaches me. His smile reveals a slightly chipped front tooth, which only adds to his attractiveness.

'Excuse me, would you mind signing my copy of your book? I'm the biggest Paige Carrigan fan going,' he says.

'I should hope so, but I go by Paige Locksley these days too.' I laugh as I kiss him: my husband and father of my child – James.

The rest of the evening speeds by in a wonderful blur of sweet fizzy wine (non-alcoholic for me), book talk, photographs, social media updates and compliments. It has been perfect.

'Ready?' asks James as the last few readers leave, all clutching signed copies of my book.

I watch them peter off, something strangely familiar about one in particular. I frown, wondering who they remind me of but as I only glimpse their retreating form, I'm unsure. Then I hear it, that tinkling laugh, accompanied by a few instantly recognisable words:

'Toodle-pip, darling!'

THE END

Also by C.L. Jennison

The Desperate Wife

What's Mine is Yours

Sunday's Child

Acknowledgements

Thank you, as always, to the brilliant team at Bloodhound Books, especially Betsy, Ian, Tara and Hannah. I continue to be such a proud and happy author within the Bloodhound kennel!

Thank you also to my wonderful husband Richard and the immediate Jennison clan, who are all so supportive of my writing career.

And it should go without saying but I'll say it anyway: thank you to each and every reader for choosing to spend your precious time with Paige. She's a character very close to my heart.

Although *More Fool Me* is my fourth published novel, it was the first full book I ever wrote, and, just like Paige's manuscript, parts of the story are based on real events. So, it's sort of a book within a book within a book in places. Very meta!

Originally titled *Her Twisted Fiction*, I chose to self-publish the first version of the book in June 2022. However, after signing with Bloodhound in September 2022, and throughout the subsequent process of publishing *The Desperate Wife*, *What's Mine Is Yours* and *Sunday's Child*, I rewrote and revised *Her Twisted Fiction* many times. Eventually, after adding a few more twists and sinister turns, it became *More Fool Me* with a warning weaved into its pages: be careful how you treat an author or you might end up in one of their novels!

A note from the publisher

Thank you for reading this book. If you enjoyed it please do consider leaving a review on Amazon to help others find it too.

We hate typos. All of our books have been rigorously edited and proofread, but sometimes mistakes do slip through. If you have spotted a typo, please do let us know and we can get it amended within hours.

info@bloodhoundbooks.com

www.ingramcontent.com/pod-product-compliance
Lightning Source LLC
Chambersburg PA
CBHW061550210726
48287CB00006B/2134